THE
EYE
OF THE
STONE

THE
EYE
OF THE
STONE

Tom Birdseye

Holiday House / New York

Library of Congress Cataloging-in-Publication Data

Birdseye, Tom.
The eye of the stone / Tom Birdseye.—1st ed.
p. cm.
Summary: When he is pulled into another world called Timmra,
Jackson finds he must fight the horrible monster Baen and
unite two warring peoples, the Faron and the Yakonan.
ISBN 0-8234-1564-3 (hardcover)
[1. Fantasy.] I. Title.

PZ7.B5213 Ey 2000
[Fic]—dc21   00-024322

This book is dedicated to my agent, Jean Naggar,
without whom . . . well, I hate to even think about it;
and to Regina Griffin,
one fine editor, indeed.

If you want to draw a bird, become a bird.

—*Hokusai*

Contents

1. A Distant Rumble

"So," Jackson Cooper muttered under his breath, "this is how I'm going to die." He leaned forward on his bicycle seat and peered over the handlebars. "Ride off a cliff the day I turn thirteen."

Jackson let out a grim laugh. No, not a cliff. He was exaggerating again. At least that's what Seth and Chris would say. It was just a little hill, nothing compared to the towering cliffs of Cougar Butte or the steep forested ridges that surrounded the small town of Timber Grove, Oregon. Twenty feet or so from Alder Street down to the gravel parking lot behind Lumberman's Hardware, that's all. No big deal, even though the narrow rutted path had turned slick with mud since the winter rains had begun.

Seth and Chris had already proved it. Without a second of hesitation they had hurled themselves off the hill's crest. Caps on backward, baggy sweatshirts billowing like sails in the cold damp air, they had plummeted straight down with no brakes, splashing with loud whoops through the big puddle at the bottom. Now they sat on their bikes looking up at Jackson, waiting.

"C'mon!" Seth called. "You said you'd do it this time!"

Jackson cringed at the all-too-familiar taunt in Seth's voice, then caught himself and recovered, forcing a grin. "I'm coming!"

Chris motioned with his hand. "Just stay to the left. Watch out for that big rock halfway down."

Jackson gave a little wave. "No problem. Almost ready!"

He closed his eyes and tired to imagine that there really *was* no problem, that he really *was* almost ready to launch himself over the edge. He wrestled the vision of it into his brain. Out of the gate—*zoom!*—barreling down the slope, fearless, laughing at the breakneck speed. A jump at the bottom, catching air like those mountain bikers on the TV ads. Muddy water flying as he slashed through the puddle. Then a quick skid sideways to a stop, throwing a clatter of gravel. Seth and Chris giving him high fives and yelling, "All right! Nice one!" The three of them riding off together, friends.

But that wistful picture vanished in a heartbeat as soon as Jackson opened his eyes and looked back down the hill again. Somehow it seemed even taller than before. And so incredibly steep, nearly vertical. An icy hollowness formed in the pit of his stomach as he imagined careening out of control, crashing into the blackberry bushes, flipping onto the jagged rocks, cut and broken. He shivered. A person really *could* die. . . .

A distant rumble shook Jackson from his morbid fantasy. Weird. The sound was sort of like thunder, but not quite. He scanned the sky. Thunder was pretty rare in November. And besides, the afternoon was only lightly overcast, a welcome break from all the days of heavy gray and relentless rain they'd been having.

The rumble came again. Deeper, more cavernous this time, it echoed off the cliffs of Cougar Butte. Or—weirder still—the sound actually seemed as if it were coming from the butte itself, as if the extinct volcano were trying to clear its throat.

"Hey, you guys," Jackson said, "what do you think is making—"

"You going to ride the hill or not?" Seth cut in. He bounced his foot impatiently on his bike pedal.

Jackson stared at Seth, then Chris. "But—But didn't you hear . . ."

3

Chris and Seth returned the stare, acting for all the world like they hadn't heard a thing.

Jackson looked back at Cougar Butte. The cliffs stood silent. He shrugged sheepishly. "I, uh . . . thought I heard something. Guess not. Funny how your ears can play tricks on you, huh? You know, make you think you heard something when really—"

"When really you're just stalling," Seth said. He shook his head. "Stalling is not a sporting event, Jackson. ESPN does not show the highlights on TV every night." He gave a sharp-edged laugh. "No one wants to watch you standing at the top of a hill for twenty minutes with your knees knocking together like a little wimp."

Jackson flinched. *Wimp.* He hated that word. Hated it. Deep in his belly it struck like a match, flared, then burst into a flame of anger that rose hot in his throat. And he wanted to scream at Seth, *Shut up! Don't say that!* At Chris, too, for not coming to his defense. *You used to be my friend!* But, as usual, he only swallowed hard and forced the bitter words back down to sit like bile in his belly.

"Stop signs rust faster than you get guts," Seth scoffed. "C'mon, Chris, he's not gonna do it. Let's get out of here." He wheeled his bike around. Chris started to follow.

The flame of Jackson's anger went out in an instant, replaced by a longing that welled up in him

4

so strong he ached. "No, don't go! I'm coming! Really!"

Chris looked back up the hill. Seth stopped, hesitated for a moment, then finally turned, too. "Well, just do it then," Seth said. "On the count of three." He nodded to Chris. Chris shrugged, then put two fingers to his mouth, ready to give the starting whistle. He had always been a great whistler.

"One!" Seth called out.

Jackson gripped the brakes of his bike so hard his knuckles turned to pale bony bumps under taut skin.

"Two!"

His heart pounded in his chest. He could hear his pulse throbbing at his temples.

"Three!" Seth shouted, and Chris let loose with a piercing whistle.

Jackson took a deep breath. *Yes, just do it!* He commanded himself. *No fear!*

But all the slick advertising slogans in the world couldn't rid him of the dread coursing through his body. No matter how loudly his mind shouted directions, his arms and legs simply wouldn't follow them. The hill was too high. He couldn't do it. Tears welled up in his eyes, a lump in his throat. For a dark moment he was sure he was going to start crying right there in front of Chris and Seth, when a horn beeped twice behind him.

Jackson jerked around to see his father's battered green pickup pulling to the side of the street. It splashed through a pothole and came to a stop beside him, the engine sputtering before it died.

A cloud of cigarette smoke billowed out into the afternoon air as the window rolled down. No, not cigarette smoke. His father was puffing on a cigar! Jackson blinked back his surprise. Since when did his father smoke cigars?

Jackson peered nervously through the blue-gray tobacco haze. Beneath the bill of a Timber Grove Lumber Company hat he could see the intense blue of his father's eyes—so familiar, and yet there was something . . . different. And not just in the eyes, come to think of it. Jackson scanned his father's face. Was it just the uncharacteristic cigar?

"I've been looking all over for you," his father said, his voice oddly flat, unreadable. "Where've you been?"

Jackson tried to ignore the unsettled feeling invading his body. He cut a quick glance down the hill toward Chris and Seth, then back. "I ran into the guys and—"

"Well, I need you to take care of Becky."

"Oh!" Startled, Jackson's hand went to his mouth. "Oh yeah. Becky." Mom had told him that they needed him to baby-sit after school. She was working a double shift at the café again, and his father had a lead on an odd job doing some remodeling for Annie Snyder. Jackson had grumbled. No one should have to baby-sit on his birthday, especially baby-sit Becky. Although only four, she could be a real pain. In the end, though, he had agreed, of course. He'd had no choice. But what time had they wanted him home? His mind raced. Three-thirty? Yes, three-thirty. Was it three-thirty already?

Jackson's father flicked cigar ashes out the truck window. They landed with an animal hiss on the wet ground. "Forgot again, didn't you?"

Jackson grimaced and offered a meek apology. "Sorry."

His father toyed with the cigar, rolling it between his thumb and forefinger. "I had to drop Becky off at the Andersons' house, which is not good. You know how she gets when she's around Jeremy and Skeeter for too long. Those boys are wild."

Jackson nodded. "Yes sir." He knew. An afternoon with Jeremy and Skeeter could turn Becky into something less than human.

Jackson's father made a noise that started as a sigh, but ended in a low, guttural growl from the back of his throat. He blinked and jerked his head, as if to shake something off, then stuck the cigar back in his mouth. "This is the third time in two weeks. *What* am I going to do with you?"

Jackson held out his hands, pleading. "I'm sorry, Dad, I promise it won't happen again. Really!"

The look Jackson got was withering. "You're darn right it won't happen again," his father snarled. He raised a beefy clenched fist. Panic rammed into Jackson's chest. But before he could even take a breath to beg for mercy, his father broke into a big toothy smile. "Not with *this* on your wrist, it won't." He opened his fist to reveal a brand-new watch in the upturned palm of his hand.

Uncomprehending, Jackson looked back and forth between the watch and his father's face. The grin there, he noticed, was strangely twisted.

"Go ahead," his father said. He offered the watch up further. "It's for you!"

Jackson stared blankly, "For me?"

His father threw back his head and laughed in what, for an instant, sounded more like someone else's voice, a strange, disturbing voice. "Yes, for you!"

"Oh," Jackson said, trying to make sense of what he was seeing and hearing. He blinked, then eyed the watch more carefully. He'd been wanting one for a long time, but no way had he actually expected to get one for his birthday. Especially from his father. Especially now. How many times had he been reminded lately about the tight family budget since the layoffs at the mill? And wasn't his father's unemployment about to run out, too? The watch looked expensive, and nice, *really* nice. Tentatively, he reached out and picked it from his father's hand.

"Check it out!" his father said. "I already set it for the right time and date—November thirteenth, your birthday! And there are lots of features, like an illuminated dial—just press that button there— and an alarm function. Cool, huh? Put it on. Put it on!"

"Um . . . all right," Jackson said. He fastened the band around his wrist, then turned it this way and that. Yes, it was cool, *very* cool.

"Whoa!" Jackson's father said. "I almost forgot. There's this, too!" He rummaged around in his shirt pocket and pulled a necklace out. He dangled it like bait before Jackson's eyes. "It's the real thing— gold links—like those pro ballplayers wear. You know, *man's* jewelry. Here, let's see how it looks." He reached out and quickly pulled the chain over Jackson's head, then tousled Jackson's hair like he hadn't done in months. "Looks great! Happy birth-day, Jackson-boy!"

Jackson didn't know what to say. What had got-ten into the man? He was acting so weird. "Uh . . . thanks," he finally managed to mumble.

"You betcha!" his father said. "Now hurry up and go over to Jeremy and Skeeter's house and get your sister. I'll be home as soon as I can. We've got lots to celebrate!" He threw back his head again and

9

laughed like a man possessed, then, to Jackson's amazement, he howled like a wolf. "Ah-ooooo! I thought it was a dream, but it's real! Lady Luck has finally come my way!"

Jackson stood dumbfounded. "Lady Luck?"

But his father just winked with a peculiar, almost demonic gleam in his eye, started the truck, revved the engine, then roared off.

It wasn't until the pickup wheeled around the corner onto Cedar Street that Jackson remembered Seth and Chris, and a smile worked its way onto his face. In addition to a new watch and a gold chain, his father had given him something else, too, without even knowing it. Jeremy and Skeeter's house was in the opposite direction from the hill. He couldn't ride down it. He was saved at the last second, just like in the movies. Saved!

Jackson's smile expanded into a full-blown grin. He covered it with his hand, though, pretending to wipe something from the corner of his mouth. He forced a look of disappointment into its place.

"I have to go," he called out as he turned back to face the boys. "Dad says I have to pick up Becky. Gotta hurry. I'm already late." He raised his new watch and pointed to it so that Seth and Chris would be sure to understand. "I really want to ride the hill. I'll do it tomorrow."

Chris shook his head in obvious disappointment. Seth cleared his throat. "Sure you will," he said, his voice dripping with sarcasm. "Wimp."

But Jackson acted like he hadn't heard. He was already pedaling as hard as he could away from the top of the hill, away from the distant rumble that called like a voice from the direction of Cougar Butte.

"Sisters!" Jackson shouted back over his shoulder. "What a pain!"

And he was gone.

2. Into the Stone

"Chocolate tastes better than boogers," Becky announced from her perch on the kitchen counter.

Jackson looked up from the peanut butter he was spreading on bread for her snack. All the way home from Jeremy and Skeeter's house, he had ignored her irritating chatter, on and on about nothing. Instead, he'd been trying to calm a nagging sense of uneasiness concerning his dad, while at the same time fighting to get that awful word—*wimp*—out of his mind.

Wimp, wimp, wimp.

He really wasn't one. Was he?

Wimp, wimp, wimp.

No. He was just sensible, that's all; careful, not a fool. Right?

Wimp, wimp, wimp.

Like he'd told Chris and Seth, he'd *had* to go get Becky. They'd seen his dad at the top of the hill. They knew. He hadn't had a choice.

Wimp, wimp, wimp.

Round and round Jackson had gone, growing more and more frustrated as he circled his own self-doubt. Which had made Becky's chatter all the more irritating.

Now, at home in the kitchen, he said, "You're disgusting. How do you know chocolate tastes better than boogers? Did you do a taste test?"

Becky wrinkled her freckled nose and shook her head. Her braids swung back and forth. "Oooo, yuck! No! Skeeter said so."

Jackson stuck the knife into the nearly empty jar and scraped a bit more peanut butter from the bottom. He spread it, then folded the bread in half— a peanut butter roll-up. Emma, their cat, curled around his legs, meowing to be fed, too. He nudged her away with his foot. "Get out of here, Emma. You've got your own food." He handed the sandwich to Becky. "So Skeeter did a taste test?"

"Uh-huh," Becky said, picking off a piece of bread crust and dropping it to Emma. "Jeremy bet him he wouldn't, but he did."

Jackson screwed the top back on the peanut butter jar and put it in the cupboard.

"Skeeter said chocolate tastes better," Becky went on. "Then he threw his boogers out the window into the yard."

That did it. The image of Skeeter shooting booger bullets was too much. Despite his mood, Jackson couldn't help smiling. "That kid is something else," he said, shaking his head. He grabbed the dirty knife off the counter and headed for the sink.

"Yep," Becky said. "Jeremy called him a wimp, but he wasn't."

Jackson stopped short. There it was again— *wimp*—now out of the mouth of a four-year-old. He flung the knife into the sink, where it clanged against a dirty pan. The word seemed to be following him around, jabbing at him from every direction. He strode to the faucet, flipped the water on high, and began to scrub at his sticky fingers. The oil in the peanut butter wouldn't wash away. He jammed the faucet off and grabbed a frayed dish towel, wiping fiercely at his hands with it.

"Skeeter's not afraid of anything," Becky said. "I bet he'd even eat cooked cauliflower. That's *lots* worse than boogers."

Jackson turned and glared at her, twisting the towel into a rat tail.

Becky took a huge bite of sandwich and grinned at him with puffed-out cheeks. "Mmm, this is good. Want some?"

"No!" Jackson shot back. "I'm going outside." He threw the towel onto the counter. "By *myself.*"

Becky nodded cheerfully and mumbled through her mouthful of food. "Awwite."

With a huff of exasperation, Jackson grabbed his Portland Trailblazers jacket off the hook and banged out the kitchen door into the damp afternoon air. He stomped down the back steps and across the yard, kicking at Becky's soccer ball, sending it ricocheting off the rusty wheelbarrow by the garage with a hollow, metallic ka-thump.

Behind the woodpile he squeezed through the hole in the fence where two boards had fallen out. Fists clinched, he leaped a moss-covered log and strode into the muted light of the forest.

Once on the narrow path that ran alongside Cougar Creek, he forced his way upstream, pushing past bracken fern and the slick glossy leaves of salal bushes, slapping at the low limbs of the vine maples and alder trees, knocking them out of his way. Deeper and deeper into the forest Jackson went, lost in his anger, until the wind gusted overhead. He looked up through the canopy of trees to see black clouds—storm clouds—scuttling across the tops of towering cliffs.

"Whoa," Jackson muttered, his indignation of a moment before quickly fading like steam from a kettle. Somehow he'd wandered all the way to the base of Cougar Butte.

Jackson shook his head. This wasn't like him, not like him at all. How long had he been walking? He checked his new watch and gasped, an instant knot forming in his stomach. Four-twenty-two! If his father got to the house and he wasn't there, he'd be in trouble, *big* trouble. Dad's earlier weird mood and generosity—whatever the bizarre reason for it—could vanish in a heartbeat, he knew, despite all the smiles and talk of dreams coming true and "Lady Luck." Birthday or not, the rules were crystal clear: He was *never* to leave Becky alone, *ever*. He'd better get home.

A cold drop of water landed with a splat on Jackson's shoulder, followed quickly by a few on his head. "Aw, man!" he moaned as the persistent patter of a steady rain began to fill the forest. He pulled his jacket collar up tight around his neck. Yes, home, *right now.*

But before Jackson could take even one step back down the path, the wind gusted again, harder this time, ripping the few remaining leaves from an alder tree and sailing them through the air in wild looping spirals. Above the bare limbs Jackson could see that the clouds had darkened even more and were swirling around the crest of Cougar Butte as if whipped by some gigantic hand. The rain grew heavy, driving down at him like icy little fists. In a matter of seconds he could feel it soaking through his jacket and shirt and onto his skin.

"Oh, great!" Jackson said aloud, trying to sound sarcastic. He began to trot but immediately tripped over an exposed tree root and went down hard. Sharp pain shot through his knee. "Ow!" He struggled to his feet again to go on, but with the first step the pain intensified and he stopped, grimacing.

It took several deep breaths, but Jackson fought back the panic he felt crawling up his back and forced the sound of confidence into his voice, as if Seth and Chris were there. "No big deal," he assured himself. "Not to worry." He looked up at the wild dark sky. "This'll let up pretty soon. Just find a place to get out of the weather for a while and rest your leg, then you can get on home."

Jackson looked around, squinting through what had become a chaos of rain and wind-whipped tree limbs. At first he saw nothing that offered shelter, but then ... there at the base of Cougar Butte, a jagged split in the rock face. If only it was big enough for him to get into.

Jackson limped his way through dripping underbrush and up a scree slope toward the butte. "Almost there," he found himself saying. "Almost there ..." Sleet mixed with the rain, stinging his face and the backs of his hands. He dropped onto all fours and climbed laboriously over the slick rocks, his knee throbbing. "Almost there . . ." Scrambling up onto a ledge, he wriggled into the crack in the cliff.

To Jackson's surprise, the opening was more than just a shallow cleft. It went deep into Cougar Butte and widened as it did so into a small cave. He peered into the blackness. An odd, discomforting smell hung in the still, dank air, like that of a match when first lit. He eased outside again. Maybe he'd be better off going down and making a run for it, after all.

A great rumbling roar shook the air. There was a splintering crack. Jackson jerked around just in time to see a slab of rock the size of a car break off Cougar Butte and come crashing down onto the slope not more than thirty feet from where he stood. He lunged back into the cave and retreated into its darkness as fast as he could, until he bumped into the back wall and could go no further. He sat down, leaning against the rock, and let out a ragged sigh of relief.

Which didn't last very long. Although out of the storm and in a dry place, his jeans and cotton shirt were completely soaked and seemed to be sucking the heat right out of him. He was already starting to shiver.

Hypothermia. Jackson knew all about it. His father had taught him. Wet, cold, and wind together caused it. First you start to shiver, just like he was doing now. Then the shivering won't stop. Pretty soon it's as if your brain has gone numb, and you start thinking crazy and are likely to do dumb things. Eventually you pass out, and then . . . Hypothermia was a killer.

Jackson bit his lower lip and forced a large swallow. An uncontrollable shudder racked him. He gingerly pulled his knees to his chest, then wrapped his arms around his legs, becoming as tight a ball as he could. He closed his eyes and tried to think warm thoughts: a tropical beach under palm trees, like in the ads; a woodstove and whistling teakettle; a bathtub full of water so hot you'd have to slip down into it an inch at a time.

Concentrating on those things, Jackson actually began to feel heat. He was about to congratulate himself on his power of concentration when he realized that the heat was not being generated by his mind, but from behind him. He turned and put his hand on the cave wall he had been leaning against. Instantly, warmth spread through his fingers and up his arm.

At another time, Jackson would have jerked his hand away. His mind would have raced with horrible thoughts: What had he stumbled onto, a lava tube like they'd studied about in science? There could be an eruption any second! Molten rock would come bursting through the cave wall! He'd die the dumbest of deaths—by fire in the middle of a sleet storm!

But at that particular moment, as cold as he was, Jackson didn't ask himself why, or how, or from what source the heat in the stone was coming. The only thing that mattered was that he was actually beginning to get warm.

Just his arm, though. The heat seemed to run out of energy below the shoulder. He needed more than that. He was cold all over. He wanted to hug a piece of the rock to him.

Jackson's eyes had adjusted to the poor light, so he could make out a small horizontal crack in the cave wall where the rock felt the warmest. He worked his fingers into it, tensed them, then gave a big tug. Nothing moved. He pulled again, harder. There was a small crunching sound. He took a deep breath, then yanked with all his might. The rock gave, and a book-sized piece of it fell onto the cave floor. Jackson reached to scoop it up, but then stopped and stared in disbelief.

Although the front side of the rock had been rough and indistinguishable from the rest of the cave wall, the back side of it—which was now lying exposed—was anything but normal. It appeared to have been hollowed out into a concave shape, much like a cupped hand. And lying in that indentation was a small, perfectly oval piece of polished black stone with a small hole through its center.

"What in the world?" Only seconds before it had been part of the cave wall. Jackson leaned closer. Etched into the surface of the black stone was what looked like a lion.

Fear shot up the back of Jackson's neck. A part of his brain began screaming, "This is weird, *really* weird. Get out of here! Run! *Now!*"

But from another part of his brain came a very different message. Not in words. It wasn't a voice, or even a thought, only a strange and yet pleasing feeling. With it Jackson's fear simply disappeared. Like fog off the mountains, it quietly evaporated, turning from something felt into something not. And just as mysteriously, something else took its place. Jackson didn't know what that something was. All he knew with sudden certainty was that everything was okay. More than okay. He reached out and picked up the stone.

Warmth flooded Jackson's palm, his arm, his entire body. The pain in his knee softened, then ceased. A sense of calm blanketed him, along with an inexplicable feeling of strength, of power. He closed his fingers tight around the stone and pressed it to his chest.

In the next instant a wild roar and blinding flash of red light exploded around him and everything seemed to tilt as if knocked off its axis. Jackson thrust his hand out, groping, grasping for something—*anything*—to hold on to. But his fingers closed on only air, and he was falling, falling. . . .

3. "Or-y-gun?"

Mud. Cold, wet, slimy. Plastered on his face. Smeared down the front of his Trailblazers jacket. Squished into his hair, cementing his curly brown locks to his scalp. The next thing Jackson knew he was sprawled in the mud.

"Ugh," he groaned. "What happened?" Only to taste mud on his tongue. "Yuck!" He pushed up onto his knees, spitting in disgust, wiping the smelly, gooey ooze from around his eyes. Cautiously opening them, he blinked in the bright light.

What Jackson saw made no sense. Instead of being in a cave in Cougar Butte, he now knelt on a tiny island of mud in the middle of a shallow river, its water gurgling by on either side.

"Huh? What the . . . ?" He must be imagining things. He squeezed his eyes shut, then opened

23

them wide. The river and island of mud were still there.

A deep, penetrating chill swept through Jackson's body. He lurched to his feet, slipped, staggered, and spun to find himself gaping up at the massive beams of a large wooden bridge arching high over his head.

Jackson looked around in wild-eyed, open-mouthed astonishment. Along one side of the river, dense stands of strange grasslike plants grew to the height of small trees. He whirled about, mud squishing beneath his feet. On the opposite side of the river stretched a field, brown earth plowed and harrowed, ready for planting. He looked up. Above it all the bright orb of the sun shone in a brilliant blue, cloudless sky.

Jackson clamped his eyes shut and kept them shut this time. No. This wasn't possible. It couldn't be. It was just a dream, an extremely strange dream, but a dream nonetheless. It *had* to be. He'd wake up any second now and it would all be over. As would the storm. So he could go home.

Yes, home. And Becky would be there, still eating her sandwich, the smell of peanut butter on her breath. She'd make some smart-aleck remark, but he would ignore her, leave her sitting there on the kitchen counter. He'd cross the living room, stepping over the dark coffee stain on the beige carpet the way he always did, then turn the corner at the bottom of the stairs. Hand on the familiar wood railing, he would look up toward his room.

That's right. He would want to be alone for a while after a dream like this. He'd climb toward his bedroom door—first one step, then two. The third step would squeak, like always. Halfway up would be the purple crayon mark on the wall, which Becky swore she didn't do. He'd gain the landing at the top, and there would be his room with the Trailblazers posters on the wall, the purple beanbag chair in the corner, the Corvette model next to the deer antler on top of his dresser, his unmade bed, and his dirty clothes on the floor. His wonderful room, all his. That was what Jackson longed for. Slowly he opened his eyes once more to see . . . river, bridge, giant grass, plowed field, sunny sky—all looking incredibly real. A warm breeze brushed his cheek, bringing with it the smell of spring.

Jackson's legs went weak, his stomach queasy. He hunched over, his hands on his knees. "What— What is happening?" he pleaded.

"I was going to ask *you*," came an urgent whisper from the bridge above him. "Is the river still going down? It's not a good sign, is it?"

Jackson bolted upright, his heart in his throat. He could see no one, only the underside of the bridge. *"Who's there?"*

"Not Father, thank goodness." It was a girl's voice, with a strange accent like none Jackson had ever heard. Her words echoed, seeming to shift from one part of his mind to another. "He's furious, says the Yakonan are to blame for all the troubles, even the earth shaking. The roof of Jal's old barn fell in this time. The village is in an uproar."

Jackson whirled to run, then whirled again. Run where?

Footsteps sounded on the bridge planks. "He and Yed have raised the banner of the Steadfast Order over the main gate. What are we going to—"

Then the girl was in Jackson's sight, leaning over the bridge railing, a look of shock on her face. "Oh! I thought you were—" she grew flustered. Fear flickered in her eyes. She looked over her shoulder, "I—I mean I was expecting—"

The girl cut herself short, took a deep breath, composed herself, then looked down again at Jackson. "You're covered with mud." She leaned farther over the bridge railing, eyeing Jackson from head to toe. "Those are *very* strange clothes."

Jackson gaped at his mud-smeared jacket, then back up at the girl. *"Strange?"* The word came out with a manic, desperate edge to it. "What's so strange about—"

Then he noticed what the girl was wearing: a long, loose-fitting cream-colored dress with a dark blue apron over it. Across her shoulders hung a maroon shawl, pinned at her throat with a large brooch. She appeared as if she had walked right off the pages of a book on ancient history.

Jackson looked around him again at what simply shouldn't be. His lower lip began to tremble. "What is going on?"

The girl tilted her head to one side. Her thick wavy hair, the color of honey, fell over her shoulder and down to her elbow. She pursed her lips. "You mean you don't know?"

"I have no idea!" Jackson blurted out. "Last thing I remember, I was in a cave at the base of Cougar Butte and—" An abrupt sob racked him. He choked it back. "Where *am* I?"

The girl's face softened. "In the Vale, of course."

"The Vale?"

The girl nodded, then motioned expansively with her hands. "Yes, home to the Timmran and Yakonan people who—"

Jackson shook his head. "But that's impossible! Just a minute ago I was in *Oregon*."

"Or-y-gun?" the girls said, stumbling over the syllables. "What is Or-y-gun?"

Jackson's answer came out in a frantic rush. "It's where I live! In Timber Grove! I was in the woods and a storm came up, and I hurt my knee, and I went into this cave and then—"

He stopped, clamping his hand over his mouth. In a sudden flash he'd realized that although he'd been thinking in English, what he'd been speaking had been something else altogether. The words had been echoing in his mind for an instant, then shifting somehow as they crossed his tongue. He stepped back, mind reeling. The girl hadn't been speaking English, either, and yet he'd understood everything she had said. This was too much, just too much. He was losing his mind.

"Could it be?" the girl murmured, her eyes filled with wonder. "I thought you were from the North, but if this Or-y-gun is just another name for the Otherworld, then . . ."

A cold sweat broke out on Jackson's forehead. "Oh, my God," he mumbled, a dizzying blur of confusion crashing over him.

"Yes, of course!" the girl exclaimed. "Dedron was right! Panenthe has answered our Prayer Song and sent you to us!"

Jackson's knees buckled. He staggered forward.

"You are the Instrument."

And everything went dark.

4. Right on the Mouth

"Here, have some Daru tea."

The voice, soft and gentle, floated through the fog in Jackson's mind. A hand touched his arm, then moved behind his head and lifted it. He tried to open his eyes but couldn't. The lids, like his entire body, felt numb, lifeless.

"It'll bring back your strength."

With great effort he tried again, and finally was able to force his eyelids halfway open. All he could make out was a small clay cup before him. Steam rose from it in wispy fingers, carrying a strange but pleasant scent.

"Drink."

The cup moved forward until it touched Jackson's lips. A tiny sip passed onto his tongue. It tasted slightly sour, but good, like hot lemonade. He swallowed. A soothing trickle of warmth glided down his throat and into his stomach.

"That's it. Have more."

The cup tilted. Jackson swallowed again, then still again as the warmth in his belly grew and began radiating out with amazing quickness, thawing the numbness first in his arms and legs, then in his fingers and toes. Up the back of his neck it went, rising like a small sun in his mind. The fog there broke, then thinned to a haze . . . and thinned more . . . until only a filmy trace of vapor remained.

"Good! You're feeling better already, aren't you? Ernt tea mixed with Daru. The combination never fails."

Jackson blinked and opened his eyes all the way to see the girl from the bridge sitting at his side, looking down at him. Panic shot through him like quicksilver. He bolted upright, a thin blanket falling from his shoulders, but he went lightheaded and fell back to the crunch and smell of straw beneath him.

Broken images flashed across his mind: being lifted out of the mud by strong arms . . . a voice, then two . . . hands steadying him through knee-deep water, helping him up the riverbank . . . stumbling along a path . . . a gate, then a door . . . whispers . . . a dark room . . . the smell of wood smoke . . . his muddy jacket gone, then back, clean . . . a warm washcloth on his brow . . . and through it all talk about things—an instrument or something—that made no sense.

Jackson shook his head. *Nothing* made any sense. "Tell me I'm not crazy," he begged. "Tell me this isn't real."

The girl's face came closer, her forehead furrowed with concern. She smoothed the blanket and tucked it under Jackson's chin. "But it *is* real. You've been sent to us, and you're in my home in the village of Timmra. And whenever you're ready we can go and you can fix the Shaw-Mara and stop the Baen from . . ."

Her words trailed off as Jackson struggled up onto his elbows, frantically looking for a way to escape, a way to get back to reality. A small fire burned on an open hearth a few feet away. From its dim, flickering light he could make out a crude table and benches built of rough-hewn planks, a wooden barrel, a clay crock, windowless walls of straw and mud, a heavy door bolted shut. He was trapped.

Fear and confusion merged in Jackson to form a desperate anger. *"What is this place?"* he demanded. It was like nothing he'd ever known. There were no signs of electricity or running water, much less a TV or phone. *"Where have you taken me?"*

The girl flinched at Jackson's harshness, but her voice held steady. "I was afraid you were getting sick, that the journey from the Otherworld had weakened you. I thought that if I brought you to my house and gave you my special teas, it would help you to rest." She tried to force a smile. "My teas are good. Dedron's mother showed me how to gather the roots, then burn the skin off in hot coals and boil the pith down. A little of the dried paste goes a long way. You've been asleep for two days."

"*Two days?*" Jackson flung the blanket onto the floor. Oh, man, was he in trouble now. Dad would kill him!

The girl's face went red. Her mouth set into a firm line. She stood and picked up the blanket. "You don't have to be rude. I was just trying to—"

"Trying to *what*?" Jackson demanded. He lunged off the straw bed and grabbed her arm. "Make me crazy? This is not real! Say it isn't! *Say it!*"

"No!" The girl jerked free of Jackson's grip, but in doing so she fell back, tripping over a bench. Spinning as she went down, she crashed against the plank table with a sharp cry. "Ow!"

Jackson's anger dissolved in a great rush of guilt. "I'm sorry. Are you all right?" He hadn't meant to shout so loud. He hadn't meant to grab her like that. "Really, I'm sorry. It's just that . . ." Tears threatened at the corners of his eyes. "It's just that I . . . I don't understand what's happening to me."

The girl clutched her side. Her voice trembled as she spoke, but there was steel in it. "What is happening is that you are the answer to our prayers. You can save everything, my life."

Jackson gawked. "Save your life? *Me?*"

The girl took a deep breath and pushed her long hair back over her shoulders, then straightened herself. Her eyes glistened with intense emotion, and for the first time Jackson noticed, even in the dim light from the fire, how incredibly blue they were, like the sky on a clear autumn day. It was as if he could see through them into her soul. And he realized that despite her nose (which was kind of big) and her freckles (he'd never liked freckles), what he saw there struck him as . . . yes, beautiful. Not beautiful like Melissa Porter at Timber Grove Middle School, not like those fashion models he'd seen on magazine covers at the Stop and Go Market, but, in some way that he couldn't put his finger on, beautiful just the same.

And she was taking one of his hands in hers. "Help us," she said, her voice now as soft and warm as her fingers. "Please."

"Uh—well," Jackson stammered. Never in his life had a girl held his hand. Girls had always acted like he didn't even exist.

The girl stood and moved close to him, her autumn-sky eyes gazing deeply into his. "You have the Power," she said, grazing his cheek with her fingertips. "I can feel it. Use it to help the people of the Vale and you'll be a great hero."

"A hero?" For a moment the image of himself as someone important, someone famous, filled Jackson's head. He could see it all: the cheering crowds, throngs of people singing his name, lines of fans begging for his autograph. He'd give anything for even just a day of that. Anything! Imagine the feeling. Just imagine. Wow!

But then, as if turning a corner to find himself facing a mirror, Jackson almost laughed aloud at his own ridiculousness. This was just more unreal craziness. A hero he was not. Never had been, never would be. He was Jackson Cooper from Oregon, not the Otherworld or wherever she thought he was from. He shook his head.

"Look," he said, "I'd like to help—"

"Wonderful!" The girl broke in, grinning with delight. "Dedron said not to give up hope! He knew!" And before Jackson could say another word, she threw her arms around his neck and kissed him right on the mouth.

5. Jackson Cooper–
Jackson Cooper

At the touch of the girl's lips, Jackson felt as if a cage door had been flung open and he'd floated out and up into the air. The fear, the anger, the heaviness of only a moment before all vanished, replaced by a lightness so startling it made him dizzy.

Could it be? Had it really happened? Had he actually been kissed? He'd spent hours dreaming that one day a girl might notice him, want to talk, *really* talk, something more than "Can I borrow a pencil?" or "What's our math homework?" He'd imagined them eating together in the cafeteria, meeting at her locker between classes, going downtown for fries at the Dairy Queen after school, or just for a walk by the river, or maybe even to a movie on the weekend. But to really actually be kissed? No matter how hard he'd tried, he'd never been able to conjure up in his mind what it might feel like. It had seemed beyond dreaming, unreal.

And yet now a lovely warm, tingly sensation lingered on his lips. He put his fingers to his mouth. It sure felt real.

Jackson blinked at the implication. But if the sensation on his lips was real, then that meant he had really actually been kissed. And if he had really actually been kissed, then that meant this particular girl had really actually kissed him. And if this particular girl had really actually kissed him, then that meant this particular girl really actually existed. And if this particular girl really actually existed, then *that* meant . . .

Jackson plopped down on the plank bench, his mind a whirlwind of wonder. He felt as if he were on a roller coaster, hurtling one moment through a dark tunnel, the next out into blinding light. At any second there could be another sudden drop or wild twisting turn.

A part of his brain kept crying, "Red alert, bozo! No way! Absolutely impossible! You've gone crazy, loony, mental, flat-out bonkers!"

But all the rest of him vibrated with a startling certainty: As unbelievable as it seemed, this particular girl really actually *did* exist. And if this particular girl really actually existed, then that meant her whole world, the Vale, really actually existed, too.

And if the Vale really actually existed, then that meant . . . well, it had to mean that he was really actually there.

Before in his life, a conclusion as wild and improbable as this would have filled Jackson with sheer panic. In a heartbeat he would have leaped to his feet and been running blind. Now, though, instead of fear, what he felt was a calm sense of clarity, an acute awareness, like nothing he'd ever experienced. And yet, at the same time, he was also filled with a surprising surge of elation, a sort of wild giddiness. He, Jackson Cooper, had been transported out of his own new-millennium world and plopped down in a *very* different other!

"Cool!" he said, shaking his head in awe.

The girl looked at him with a question in her eyes. "No, it's warm today. Why do you say it's cool?" She shrugged. "Whatever the weather, it doesn't matter to me. *You* are what matters. You're here, and it makes me feel like . . ." A dazzling smile spread across her face. "It makes me feel like dancing!" She grabbed his hands and playfully pulled him into the center of the room. "Would you dance with me?"

Jackson shrank back. He didn't know how to dance. What if he made a fool of himself, stepped on her toes, or fell down? Just the thought of such a humiliation knotted his stomach.

But then the girl began to sing, her voice soft and serene, a lilting wordless melody so soothing that the tension in his stomach instantly melted away. His thoughts floated with the notes of her song as if he were in a dream where he imagined walking with her under a beautiful night sky. In his mind, the stars winked down at them from a domed ceiling of blackness so deep it seemed to vibrate. All around, torches were being lit, first one, and then another, creating a warm pool of light. Musicians sat to one side, holding wooden flutes and pipes of a kind Jackson had never seen.

One of the flute players sounded a note as soft and serene as the girl's voice. Another answered the call with a trio of rising tones. Higher pitches joined in, then the lumbering bass pipes beneath it all, until they all burst, clear and strong, into lively song.

Suddenly couples materialized out of nowhere, all dressed in flowing clothes, spinning and twirling, moving side by side with the music like a school of fish in a familiar stream. And this time when the girl held out her hand, instead of being afraid, Jackson confidently took it. He pulled her to him and danced with her to the music like he'd once seen a handsome man dance with a beautiful woman in a romantic movie. Round and round the two of them whirled in the warm torchlight, the scent of the girl filling him as if he had inhaled spring.

"You smell like flowers," Jackson said, the words spilling out as quickly as he thought them. And the next thing he knew, the trance-like dream was broken and he was back in the girl's house again within closed walls. She was looking up at him with her mouth hanging open.

Jackson went beet-red with embarrassment. *Smell like flowers? What a nitwit thing to say.* "Uh . . . w-well—" he stammered, "what I meant was—" He stepped back. "I'll bet you always smell—uh—*no*, not smell, but—" He was starting to panic. "Um, what I *really* meant was—uh, that you're—you're *beautiful*."

The girl's eyes went watery, and Jackson thought he had really stuck his foot in his mouth. It was probably an insult in this place she called the Vale to compliment someone like that, no matter how true it might be.

But then her face melted into that dazzling smile again. "Do you really think so? No one has ever said that to me before."

Now Jackson was as baffled as he had been nervous. "You've got to be kidding."

The girl shook her head. "No. Neither Timmran nor Yakonan men say such things, but—oh, you *are* a gift!"

Jackson grinned with both relief and delight. A gift. She'd called him a gift! Like he'd heard someone say, "God's gift to women!" He puffed his chest out, reveling in the thought. Man, did it feel good to be talked to like that!

The girl hurried past Jackson. "We must celebrate!" she exclaimed.

"Huh?" Startled, Jackson jerked around. "Celebrate what?"

"Arnica!" The girl strode to a small door Jackson hadn't noticed in the back of the room and flung it open. "Arnica, come see!"

A little girl with blond braids looked up from her work at a crude loom made of lashed branches. "He's all right, then?" she asked, eyes as wide as her smile. "Oh, good." And she was up and running from the little alcove into the main room, skidding to a stop only inches from Jackson's feet. "My name is Arnica," she said, bouncing up and down on her toes. "*I* am Tessa's sister!"

"Tessa?" Jackson shifted from one set of sparkling blue eyes to the other. So the first girl ever to kiss him was named Tessa.

Tessa's hand went to her mouth. "Oops, sorry. I forgot to introduce myself. My name is Tessandrica, like the wild flowers that grow in the spring. But everyone just calls me Tessa."

"That's because she's just wild, not a flower," Arnica said with a giggle.

Tessa scowled. "I am *not* wild." She pushed Arnica, but there was playfulness in it.

Arnica giggled even louder and pushed her sister back. "Yes, you are. Father and Yed say—"

"Enough of me and my sister," Tessa cut in. She turned back to Jackson. "What's *your* name?"

"My name?" It suddenly occurred to Jackson that in this new world he could be somebody different from what he'd always been—a new man, so to speak. Why not have a new name? He could make one up. . . .

But as he looked from Tessa to Arnica and back to Tessa again, the impulse left him as quickly as it had come. No way was he going to lie to the first girl who'd ever kissed him, or to her little sister. He cleared his throat and said his real name with new-found pride.

"Jackson Cooper."

Tessa pursed her lips and nodded. "Jackson Cooper." Then she repeated his name. "Jackson Cooper. It has the sound of—"

"Jackson Cooper–Jackson Cooper!" Arnica sang with glee, turning it into a little tune. "Jackson Cooper–Jackson Cooper, Jackson Cooper–Jackson Cooper!"

Tessa glared. "Just Jackson Cooper, not Jackson Cooper–Jackson Cooper. You listen too little and talk too much."

Arnica's smile dropped like a stone. "I'm sorry." She turned to Jackson. "I didn't mean to be rude."

"It's OK," Jackson said, fighting back a chuckle. "Don't worry. I don't mind."

Arnica nodded but still looked upset. She stuck the end of her long braid in her mouth and began to suck on it like a baby would a thumb.

Tessa let out a puff of aggravation. "How many times do I have to tell you not to eat your hair? If you're hungry, get yourself some stew, as well as some for Jackson Cooper, whose name you like to say so much."

Arnica glanced over her shoulder toward the big door at the front of the room. "But Father and Yed aren't here, and they always say that—"

"Father and Yed say many things," Tessa said, eyes narrowing for a moment. But then her face softened. "We have an important guest." She looked at Jackson. "*Very* important. We eat whenever we choose."

"Oh!" Arnica tossed her braid over her shoulder and bounced up on her toes, delight back in her eyes. "What fun!"

Tessa prodded her sister with her elbow. "It would be even *more* fun if you went and served some food. Hurry! We've got lots to do!"

Arnica nodded. "Yes. Yes!" She ran to a big iron pot hanging from a tripod over the open hearth and lifted the lid. A wonderful earthy aroma wafted toward Jackson, and suddenly he realized that he was so hungry it felt as if he hadn't eaten in days.

Three helpings of savory venison stew later, Jackson pushed back from the table with a sigh of satisfaction. If anything proved that all of this was indeed real, the food did. No way could you imagine a flavor as delicious as that, or a full belly and the feeling of contentment that came with it.

Sure, there were still a ton of things he didn't understand about the Vale: where it was and when, how he got there and why. It seemed that the black stone he'd found in the cave in Cougar Butte had to have had something to do with it. After all, as soon as he'd picked it up, things had started to get weird.

Jackson slipped his hand between the two top buttons of his shirt and cradled the smooth oval in his fingers. How it had gotten strung onto the gold chain his father had given him, he had no idea. Had he done that, or maybe Tessa, at some point he couldn't recall? When he was feeling so woozy? Now it hung from the chain like a pendant. Which was nice, come to think of it. It made the stone easy to touch.

With his fingertips he traced the drawing of the lion etched into the stone's surface. Or was it a lion? The grooves felt somehow different than he remembered. He couldn't really see the carving while he was wearing it. He tilted his head, trying to get a better look, but the chain was too short. Which seemed odd. Hadn't it fit easily over his head when his dad had first put it on him?

The thought of his father, then Becky, then his mom and home, surfaced in Jackson's mind and began to nag at him. What in the world was he doing just sitting there acting like all of this was normal? He should be doing everything in his power to get himself back to Timber Grove.

But just as quickly as the concerns surfaced, they faded away, and Jackson found himself shrugging. Everything was okay in Timber Grove. Somehow he just knew it. No need to worry. He was right where he was supposed to be, there in the Vale. He ran his fingers over the black stone one more time, then picked up his wooden spoon and scraped the last bit of the thick, rich stew sauce out of the corner of the bowl. Mmm, was it ever good! He could easily get used to that kind of cooking.

Jackson smiled. Funny, but it seemed like he already *was* used to it, used to everything. What had started out as the most bizarre and confusing nightmare imaginable had somehow come to feel downright natural, as if he'd been there for months or years. Actually, when he thought about it, it seemed as if he'd known this place and these people—

especially Tessa—his whole life. Everything felt so meant to be, so . . . well, it just felt so *right*.

And no wonder! He'd never had such a big deal made over him. He'd been kissed, sung to, danced with, waited on hand and foot, fed like a hero, treated like a king! Who needed a TV or a telephone? If he could just have another cup of that good Ernt and Daru tea, life would be pretty close to perfect.

He turned toward the hearth to ask for seconds, only to see a tall, muscular young man—maybe eighteen years old—standing in the doorway to the weaving alcove. In his powerful hands he held a bow with an arrow notched to the string.

The arrow was pointed straight at Jackson.

6. A Hole in Time

Jackson's heart went to his throat.

"Don't move," the bowman said, his deep voice as steady as the arrow aimed at Jackson's heart.

Jackson didn't even breathe. His eyes were riveted to the sharp tip of the arrowhead, which gleamed black and shiny in the firelight.

Arnica, however, spun around from where she sat by the hearth and leaped to her feet, a big grin on her face. "Yed! I didn't hear you come in." She started to run to him, but he barked, "Stop!" and she halted as if hit. Face stricken, she quickly bowed. "I'm sorry. I forgot."

Eyes and arrow still trained on Jackson, Yed let out a slow sigh. "How many times do I have to tell you, little sister? Father is now Radnor, Chieftain of Timmra. And I am heir to the Chieftain's Chair. You have to show him, and *me,* the respect that comes with our positions." He glanced around the room. "Where's Tessa?"

Jackson glanced around, too. Yes, where *was* Tessa? She'd been there only minutes before. He peered into the weaving alcove. It was empty. There must be a back door he didn't know about. She'd slipped out when he was busy eating. But why hadn't she told him she was leaving and when she'd be back? He wanted her there, *really* wanted her there, *right then.*

"Oh, Tessa," Arnica said. "She's gone to—" But then she stopped short and shook her head.

"Gone where?" Yed demanded.

Anxiety flickered across Arnica's face. She looked down and began to fidget with her braid, twisting it around her index finger. "Um . . . gone to tell—to do as Fa—uh, Radnor—ordered. To . . . uh, get deer antler from Gibron so that she can make more combs for the Market of Vale."

Yed studied his little sister for a long moment as she untwisted her braid, then twisted it back again.

"We won't be trading combs or anything with the Yakonan anymore," he finally said, his face grim. "The voice of Zallis came to Radnor again, right after the earth shook. It told him that the Yakonan are to blame for the troubles." He eyed Jackson for a moment. "There's to be no contact with them at all. It's now law, Radnor's Decree. Do you understand?"

"Yes, Yed," Arnica said meekly, and bowed again.

"And you're not to say 'the Vale' or 'the Market of Vale' anymore, either. It's Timmra, so we say 'the Market of Timmra.' That's the law, also. Is that clear?"

Arnica bowed yet again. "Yes, Yed."

Yed nodded, his blond curls bobbing over his eyebrows. "Good. We'll need to make sure Tessa understands, too, and follows them." Again he eyed Jackson, then lowered his bow and took the black-tipped arrow from the string. Slipping the arrow into a leather quiver, he leaned both against the wall near the hearth.

Jackson let out a silent sigh of relief, but cut it short when Yed glowered at him and patted a dagger sheathed at his waist. The message rang as loud and as clear in Jackson's mind as if Yed had shouted it: Mess with me and I'll carve you into little pieces. That conveyed, Yed turned back to Arnica and gently said, "Come here, little one."

Arnica did as instructed, standing before her big brother with head lowered.

"I know it is hard with Mother gone," Yed said, laying a brawny hand on Arnica's small shoulder. "But with the help of Zallis we can be strong." He leaned down and gave her a kiss on top of the head. "You're all right, then?"

Arnica looked up. "Yes, Yed, I'm fine."

A hint of a smile played around the corners of Yed's mouth. "Go and help Tessa, then. I need a word with this . . . this newcomer I've heard rumors about."

He swung his attention once again to Jackson, and for the first time Jackson noticed the color of Yed's eyes. They were the same vibrant blue as Tessa's and Arnica's, but carried a sharpness that penetrated like a lance. Jackson flinched as they leveled on him.

Arnica seemed not to notice, all brightness and smiles once more, as if she hadn't been equally tense only a moment before. "Oh, I know his name!" she announced with pride. "And Tessa says he has power, like *magic*, I guess, and—" She stopped short again, obviously flustered.

"Magic?" Yed said. He looked Jackson over with increased intensity. "He doesn't look like he'd have magic. He's too young, and too small. Only Radnor has magic. He can hear the voice of Zallis." He turned back to Arnica. "What else did Tessa say?"

"Oh." Arnica grew even more anxious. She picked up her braid and twisted it into a tight coil again. "She . . . um, I don't remember exactly—"

Yed's eyebrows went up. "Don't remember?"

Arnica stuck her braid in her mouth and gave a pathetic little shrug.

Yed shook his head and rolled his eyes. "Never mind. I'll find out who he is for myself." He shooed her off with his hand. "Now go and do as I said."

"Yes, Yed." Relief showing plainly, Arnica scurried past Yed toward the weaving alcove, but she stopped in the doorway. "His name is Jackson Cooper–Jackson Cooper," she whispered back.

Then she was gone.

Yed's piercing gaze leveled on Jackson yet again. "Jackson Cooper–Jackson Cooper," he said slowly, as if gauging the weight of each syllable on his tongue.

"Hi," Jackson said, trying to deepen his voice like Yed's, make it seem friendly and yet manly, too, self-assured. His words came out more like an apology than a greeting, though; more wimpy than confident. "But actually, uh . . . it's not Jackson Cooper–Jackson Cooper, it's just—uh—Jackson Cooper."

Yed frowned. "Jackson Cooper," he said, and Jackson was struck by how different his name sounded on Yed's tongue than it had on Arnica's and Tessa's—as if it were a stick with which to probe for weaknesses. Jackson shifted on the bench, suddenly aware of the rough-hewn board beneath him.

For the long moment that followed, Yed said nothing. He continued looking into Jackson's eyes, holding them in his gaze. Other than the occasional pop of a log on the fire, the room was quiet—much too quiet for Jackson's liking.

"Arnica says you have magic," Yed said, finally breaking the silence. Disbelief rang clear in his voice. "What kind of magic?"

Jackson squirmed under Yed's gaze. "Uh . . ." He gave a sheepish shrug. "Well, actually—"

"Show me," Yed said. "Is that a thing of magic?" He pointed a strong, calloused finger at Jackson's wrist.

Jackson looked at the new digital watch his father had given him. "You mean this?" Despite the situation, he almost smiled. Surely this guy wasn't serious.

Yed crossed his arms over his chest, looking as serious as anybody Jackson had ever met in his entire life. Only then did it dawn on him: Yed actually had no idea what a watch was!

But come to think of it, was that such a surprise? With no electricity or running water and only a fire to cook over, small wonder these people didn't have watches. They probably had no modern technology at all in the Va—uh, he'd better get this right if it was the law—in Timmra.

The reminder of where he was ran through Jackson's mind like cold little feet, and for an instant the urge to run swept through him.

Yed's voice took on an insistent edge. "Is that a thing of magic or not?" The question was every bit a demand. "If so, what is its purpose?"

"Its purpose? Uh . . . " Jackson tried to focus on an answer. "Well, I guess—um, well—" He fumbled for words. How do you explain a watch to someone who's never seen one? To plunge ahead seemed the only way. "It's called a watch. It's for keeping track of time. The numbers tell you what hour and minute it is, and the day and the month, so like if you . . ." He had to stop and think for a moment. "So like if you're out somewhere and you need to get home at a certain time, like for dinner, it'll tell you when to go."

Yed's laugh was so sudden and sharp it made Jackson jump. "I need nothing to tell me when to go home for dinner," Yed said. "I have eyes. I can see. As the sun sets, I go. That thing—What did you call it? A watch?—it's not magic. It's just silly!"

Normally, with a bigger, older guy towering over him like that, Jackson would have just agreed. *Yes, it's silly. Really silly. Ridiculously silly. Sorry. Beg your pardon. Don't hurt me—please.*

But now he felt a warm sensation in his chest and neck and reached up to find that it was coming from the stone pendant. Without question or hesitation he grasped the black oval, and a sudden sense of calm came over him. He took a deep breath and raised up in his seat.

"Yeah, but where I come from in Oregon, time is very important. The *exact* time," he said in a voice so firm and confident it surprised him. "With this . . . magic watch of mine, I know the hours and the minutes *and* seconds, even if it's dark. It has an illuminated dial." He offered the watch up for Yed to view, pushing the tiny silver button on its side the way his father had shown him. "There are the numbers, see? Right now the time is exactly—"

"*Eh?*" Yed gasped. "It glows like— You've captured the fire of Zallis!" He leaned close, mouth hanging open in obvious amazement.

Jackson hardly noticed. Although the dial light on his watch was working, the time reading was not. It showed 4:43 P.M., the date November 13, his birthday. Four-forty-three must have been about when he'd gone into the cave at the base of Cougar Butte.

But Tessa had said he'd been asleep for two days. And it seemed like so much had happened since then. How long had he been in Timmra altogether, anyway? Time definitely seemed different there, almost as if operating under another set of rules. It really did feel like he'd been there all his life, and yet his watch had not advanced at all. Which must mean that not only had he been transported to another place, he'd been transported through a hole in time as well. He shook his head in wonder.

"Wow!"

Yed leaned even closer, his face now more like an excited child's than the heir to the Chieftain's Chair. "What is *wow*? Is it filled with magic, too, like this on your arm? Is it a magic word?" He eagerly pulled up a stool and sat down beside Jackson. "How much of this kind of magic is there in this place you come from, this Or-y-gun? I want to know. I want to know *everything*!"

7. The Prophecy

"Incredible!" Yed jumped from his seat and began pacing back and forth in front of the hearth. "So with one of these things called a gun, you can shoot from far away!"

"*Very* far," Jackson said. He still wasn't quite sure how they had gotten onto the subject of weapons. Yed's questions had come in what seemed like an endless string. He lapped up answers like a puppy does milk, and then he wanted more, *more*. From where they had started—with his watch and its illuminated dial—they had leaped to electricity, to lightbulbs, back to electricity (very hard to explain), to cars, to airplanes, to computers (*impossible* to explain), to TV, to video games, then somehow to guns.

"Such magic!" Yed exclaimed. He picked up his bow and looked it over. "So much more powerful than this!"

Jackson smiled, basking in the limelight of Yed's attention. Okay, so maybe he was fudging a bit, letting Yed think that his watch was magical, that everything from Oregon was magical.

But if you really considered it, what was magic, anyway? A mystery, right? He had no idea how a computer actually worked. Or a digital watch. Or a TV. Or a gun. They were all mysteries. So, in a way, they all had a sense of magical power about them.

Especially a gun. Just last December, while looking for hidden Christmas presents, Jackson had discovered a pistol in the back corner of his father's top dresser drawer. The sight alone of the black leather holster lying in a nest of balled-up work socks had instantly set his heart to pounding. He could get in big trouble just for being there, rummaging around in his father's dresser, much less for looking at the gun. He almost slammed the drawer shut and raced from the room.

But then he noticed the pistol handle sticking out of the holster. It was made of beautiful, tight-grained wood that had been varnished and polished to a deep sheen. A crosshatched grid pattern had been etched into the sides for better grip. It seemed to say, "Pick me up. Hold me." And before Jackson knew it, he had lifted the gun from the drawer and pulled it from the holster.

Jackson turned the gun in his hand, testing the weight, the feel. It was heavier than he'd expected and had a slight smell of oil. He ran his fingers over the smooth blue-black metal of the barrel. On its side was engraved RUGER GP .357 MAGNUM CAL. Even the name sounded powerful.

But of course a gun was nothing without bullets. Surely his father didn't keep the pistol loaded. Better check, though. A small button near the cylinder looked promising. He'd seen enough guns to know it wasn't the trigger. He pushed it and the cylinder clicked loose, flipping out to the side. All six chambers were empty.

Jackson looked back in his father's sock drawer. A small box rested to one side of where the gun had lain. Printed on it were the words *Ultramax .357, Semi Wad Cutters*. He lifted the box out, opened the end flap, and peered inside. Like little rockets, the shells stood on end, brass cartridges stuck in holes in a plastic tray, silver bullets pointed up, ready for blastoff. At least half were gone, had already been fired.

The image of his father holding the gun filled Jackson's mind—the sinewy hand wrapped around the handle, raising the barrel with a cool slowness, thick finger on the trigger, aiming . . . at what? Jackson could almost hear the sharp crack of the shot, the sudden thud as each missing bullet slammed into any number of possible targets. Once he'd seen his dad blast three pop cans in a row off the back fence. *Blam! Blam! Blam!*

Jackson began to pull one shell after another from the box, inserting them into the chambers—four, five, six, loaded. He spun the cylinder gunfighter style, like he'd seen in those old Clint Eastwood Westerns they'd rented at the video store. Then he pushed it back up into place. It closed with an exact click, ready to fire. He raised the pistol and squinted down the barrel, taking aim at the lamp on the dresser. He popped his tongue against the roof of his mouth and said, "Blam! Gotcha!"

A thrill surged through Jackson's body, a sensation like none he'd ever had. He held control of life and death in his hands, and yet he—Jackson Cooper, whom Seth had called a wimp so many times—wasn't even frightened, not one little bit.

As a matter of fact, the gun had felt . . . well, it had made him feel equal to Seth, or Chris, or *anyone,* for that matter. There had been a strength in possessing it, even for those few short minutes he had dared to hold it in his hands; a sort of . . . yes, a sort of magical power.

"I should have known!" Yed exclaimed, clapping himself on the forehead with the palm of his hand. "The prophecy!" He strode from the hearth over to

Jackson and gave him a good-natured slap on the back. "Radnor said Zallis told him you would come to help us in our time of trouble!"

"Huh?" Jackson felt a sudden tinge of uneasiness. "What? Help you?" As much as it had become important to him to gain Yed's approval, maybe he shouldn't have gone on quite so much. "But how could I—"

"Come on!" Yed said, pulling Jackson to his feet as if he weighed nothing. "We've got to show Radnor!"

Jackson gaped. "Show Radnor? But isn't he—"

"The Chieftain of All Timmra," Yed declared, "and Commander of the Steadfast Order!"

"The Steadfast Order?"

But the growing line of questions in Jackson's mind never had a chance to advance as Yed swept him out the front door.

8. The Hall of the Steadfast Order

Yed and Jackson emerged, as if out of a cocoon, into bright afternoon sunshine and warm air. Jackson stood blinking at a large open village square full of canopied market stalls and teeming with men, women, and children, each and every one in motion. That is, until a ruddy-faced man in a green tunic who was leading a horse-drawn cart noticed him. The man stopped and stared, then reached out and tapped the shoulder of a tall fellow with a long ponytail who was unloading large bundles of firewood onto the hard-packed dirt. The first man whispered to the second, who in turn got the attention of a harried-looking woman, who in turn hushed her two squabbling children. In only a matter of seconds, everyone in the square had stopped and was staring at Jackson. "There he is," murmured the crowd. "That's the one!"

Jackson stepped back. At Timber Grove Middle School, whispers were used to plan ridicule before it became public. He braced himself for laughter, scorn, or worse. Like Yed, most of the men carried a weapon of some kind—bow, sword, dagger. A few carried all three.

Yed leaned close, "Don't worry. They can see that even with your strange clothes, you are not the enemy. You were made in the same image as us."

Jackson surveyed the crowd. True enough. If he just concentrated on the faces that stared at him, he could see that they were, in fact, a lot like his own. Some seemed quizzical, others friendly, even respectful. One child looked up at him in what appeared to be open awe. But not one pair of blue eyes showed any anger, hostility, or contempt. No sword or dagger had been drawn, no arrow fitted to bowstring.

Yed gave Jackson a gentle nudge. "Let's take the shortcut. We should get to Radnor as quickly as possible." He guided Jackson away from the open stares of the people in the square and into a narrow alley.

Mud-and-straw houses lined both sides, the eaves of their thatched roofs hanging low, just above Yed's head. As they walked, Jackson could see that behind each dwelling, stone fences divided the land into small plots. In one stood a large pig, snorting as it rooted in the mud. Another held goats; yet another, a cow and three squawking chickens. Several horses were corralled in a larger area, one of which raised its head and whinnied.

A rooster crowed. From a nearby house came the cry of a baby, then the soothing sound of a mother singing. The clank of metal on metal echoed in the distance. Jackson's head filled with the smells of wood smoke, damp earth, barnyard, and—

"Ah, roast stag!" Yed said, sniffing the air. "My favorite! After everything is settled, we should go up into the Barrier Mountains and hunt together." He draped his arm over Jackson's shoulders. "What do you think?"

Jackson didn't know what to say. For as long as he could remember, he'd dreamed of the day his father would teach him how to shoot, then take him hunting. But only a week before he finally turned twelve—the age his parents had agreed that he'd be old enough to try for his first deer—the mill had announced the layoffs and . . . well, it just hadn't been the time to ask.

But now here was Yed offering freely what had come to seem so unattainable in Timber Grove. Jackson searched Yed's face for signs. Was this a cruel joke like the ones Seth enjoyed playing? Bait and then strike? Turn it all on its head with sarcasm and ridicule? He hoped not, really hoped not. He wanted to believe it was all sincere. Still, experience had bred caution.

"Here we are!" Yed said. "The Hall of the Steadfast Order." Stopping before a large wooden door in a stone wall, he thrust his right hand in front of his eyes, then drew it slowly away as he looked upward.

Jackson followed Yed's gaze. Directly above them, jutting out like a crude porch roof, was a platform of lashed branches. On it lay a dead ram, its limp neck draped over the edge, its tongue—red with blood—hanging out.

Jackson took a quick breath. "Why is *that* there?" The glassy eyes of the ram held his own in a fixed stare. He felt both repulsed and fascinated at the same time.

Yed turned to Jackson with a baffled expression. "It's our sacrifice, of course. Surely you know—" He stopped and ran his fingers through his blond curls, peering into Jackson's eyes. "You've been through a lot getting here to Timmra, haven't you?"

Jackson blinked and looked away from the dead ram. "You can say that again."

Yed's eyebrows went up in surprise. "Why would I repeat myself? A man's words should stand strong the first time spoken." But then he shrugged. "If you need anything said again, Jackson Cooper,

I'll do it." And with that he stepped under the dead ram and rapped his knuckles on the door.

There was the sound of footsteps, then a clank of metal as the bolt slid to one side. The door swung back. In the opening stood a large, fierce-eyed man, burly as a bear, with a bushy blond beard. His hand rested on the hilt of a great broadsword.

Yed stood stiff at attention, his body taking on a sudden formalness, as did his voice. "Radnor," he said, "Chieftain of All Timmra and Commander of the Steadfast Order." Then he bowed.

Although not used to bowing, Jackson quickly followed suit. There was something about Radnor that demanded it. Jackson's eyes came down to the level of Radnor's sword hilt. From that close he could see that the top knob had been carved into the shape of a clenched fist much like Radnor's own thick fingers and broad knuckles. Everything about Radnor, Chieftain of All Timmra and Commander of the Steadfast Order, exuded power.

Jackson bowed even farther. The stone pendant that hung from his neck swung out of the top of his shirt. He reached up and gripped it for a moment.

From above came a voice like gravel. "Rise."

Jackson stood upright to find Radnor's blue eyes boring into his. He almost looked away, but the warmth from the stone lingered, as did the sudden, mysterious sense of calm. He straightened his shoulders and held Radnor's gaze.

Radnor nodded. "Enter."

"We enter," Yed said, leading Jackson past the big man into a dim foyer. A lone torch flickered in its mount on the wall. The tart smell of burning pine pitch filled the smoky air. Beyond the foyer Jackson could barely make out the opening of a hallway. He peered down it but couldn't see what lay beyond. No light came from within.

"This is Jackson Cooper," Yed said to his father.

Jackson turned to see Yed motioning toward him. The formalness, he noticed, was gone from Yed's body and voice now that they were inside and the door to the alleyway was closed. Yed leaned close to his father. "I know it's not my position to decide," he said. "You alone can hear the voice. But I think he might be the One. He has magic."

Radnor's eyes fixed on Jackson's again. "Magic? What kind of magic?"

Yed smiled. "Show him the watch, Jackson Cooper. Look there, Radnor, on his wrist."

Radnor bent down to examine Jackson's wrist. "But I don't see any—"

"The other wrist," Yed said with a gentleness that startled Jackson. In Timber Grove no teenage boy would be caught dead talking that way to his father—not in front of anyone, anyway. It was the tone of voice used by little boys.

Yed put his hand affectionately on his father's shoulder and pointed to Jackson's watch. "There, on that strap."

For a second Jackson thought he saw a hint of a wry smile beneath Radnor's thick beard. "Of course." The big man leaned close as Jackson offered his left wrist.

Yed prodded Jackson. "Now show him. Show him the fire."

Jackson looked at Yed, then at Radnor. What harm could it do? Yed had gotten such a big kick out of it. "Okay," he said, and pushed the button that illuminated the watch dial.

Radnor's eyebrows went up in surprise at the green glow. "Ehhhhh?"

Yed smiled. "But that is nothing. Wait until you hear about . . ." And with that he went on to detail every single thing Jackson had told him of the magical wonders of Oregon.

Several times during Yed's grand recital, Jackson found himself thinking that he should interrupt and try to set things straight, explain what Oregon really was, and where. And that all the things Yed spoke of were just inventions, technology, ordinary stuff in Timber Grove. And that he was just Jackson Cooper with a new watch, not the something special they seemed to want him to be.

But the simple truth was that Jackson was enjoying listening to Yed go on and on about him too much to cut the telling short. It felt incredibly good to hear himself praised. By the time Yed finished—"And with this thing called a gun, you can shoot from a great distance!"—Radnor, Chieftain of All Timmra and Commander of the Steadfast Order, was looking at Jackson with great appreciation. That felt even better.

"Just as it was spoken to me!" Radnor said with a huge smile. "Welcome to Timmra, Jackson Cooper! Welcome, indeed!"

Jackson grinned. No way was he going to admit that he'd never even pulled the trigger of his father's pistol—he'd been too afraid—much less hit something, especially at a great distance. "Thank you," he said, and bowed to Radnor.

"He's come just in time, don't you think?" Yed said.

"Yes," Radnor replied, "but I've been given no instructions. . . ." His expression grew serious. He stroked his beard for a moment, then closed his eyes and gently placed his powerful hand over them. "Let me understand," he said. He slowly drew his hand away to reveal his eyes open again, locked in a fixed stare off into the darkness of the hallway.

Jackson looked at Yed for an explanation of what Radnor was doing. But Yed put his finger to his lips, signaling Jackson not to interrupt. Yed closed his eyes and waited in silence. Not wanting to offend, Jackson did the same. The foyer of the Hall of the Steadfast Order grew quiet, save the sizzle of the pine-pitch torch mounted on the wall.

After a long moment, Radnor finally stirred, and Jackson opened his eyes to see the chieftain shaking his head as if coming out of a trance.

"To the armory," Radnor said. "First, we must get Jackson Cooper a bow."

Yed's eyes popped open. "A bow? But I thought—"

"So it has been spoken to me," Radnor said.

Without a blink, Yed nodded. "Then so it must be."

9. Among Friends

Radnor grabbed the torch from its holder on the foyer wall and led Jackson and Yed into the dark hallway beyond. No one spoke; the only sound was the scuff of their feet on the stone floor. They rounded a corner and the walls seemed to close in on either side, the air to grow musty. A large wooden door with heavy wrought-iron hinges and bolts loomed ahead.

"Open it," Radnor told Yed.

Yed unbolted the door at the top and the bottom, then grabbed the thick iron handle with both hands and looked over his shoulder at Jackson. "Feast your eyes on the work of Radnor!" he called out as if hundreds had gathered. With a great heave he swung the door open to reveal in the torchlight a long narrow room, lined on both sides with an arsenal of weapons: swords, spears, shields, and enough bows and quivers of arrows to supply a small army.

Jackson gawked. He loved bows, always had. One hung above the couch at home in Timber Grove, next to the mounted head of a six-point buck. His father had made the bow out of ash wood long before Jackson was born. For reasons that were never made clear, at no time had Jackson been allowed to touch it. That had somehow made the bow seem even nicer, like a museum piece, hanging there out of reach, looking perfect.

Here, though, there were dozens of them, each one far nicer than his father's, truly perfect in every detail—recurved on the ends, intricately carved designs above the carefully wrapped leather hand-grips, sanded and polished to a bright sheen.

"You made them *all*?" Jackson asked Radnor, noticing one bow in particular with a carving of a great stag on it.

A flush of embarrassment crossed Radnor's face. "Yed likes to exaggerate," he said. "The truth is—"

"That he is a very good bow maker," Yed finished for his father.

"Praise no bow before it's tested," Radnor said trying to sound stern. He faked a scowl but couldn't hide his pride, so waved Yed off with his hand. "Talk, talk, talk. It seems my son was born to pester me like a talking fly."

Yed reached over and plucked a piece of lint from his father's beard. "It's my duty," he said, a mischievous glint in his eyes. He let the lint float to the floor. "I may not be able to split a melon at fifty paces or shoot an arrow through a bird's eye, but I'm quick with my tongue."

Radnor laughed openly. "Unfortunately, this is all too true."

"Just as it's true that you are a very good bow maker," Yed insisted. He whispered loudly to Jackson, "Not only did he make most of them, he also straightened and hardened the arrows, too, forged the points, *and* mounted the feathers."

Radnor ignored his son's boasting. "Which bow do you like, Jackson Cooper?"

Jackson stared. "Do you mean I can use one of these?"

Radnor shook his head. "No."

Jackson's shoulders slumped.

"I mean you may *have* whichever one you choose. So it is spoken."

"Easy now," Radnor whispered into Jackson's ear some time later. "Calm yourself before letting the arrow go." His rumbling voice was as steady as he was asking Jackson to be.

Jackson strained to hold the bow with the stag carving still. He squinted down the arrow shaft at his target—a black circle of dirt rubbed into the center of a piece of stiff leather. It leaned against a large mound of hay piled in the high stone-walled enclosure behind the armory. Six shots had already flown high and wide to the left, burying themselves in the hay.

Yed's voice came at Jackson from the other side. "Think the arrow to its mark, Jackson Cooper."

Jackson's arms began to quiver. The strain of holding the bowstring back was quickly taking its toll. Sweat trickled over his temples and down the sides of his face.

"Relax," Radnor said. "Breathe in, then halfway out, then release. It's the Way."

Jackson forced all of his concentration into what he was doing. It had become very important to him to do well, to look good in both Radnor's and Yed's eyes. Not in the same way he had always wanted Chris's and Seth's approval. That was out of fear of their teasing, their ridicule. This was differ-ent. Radnor and Yed were . . . well, really nice and patient with him. It seemed as if they wanted him to succeed, where Chris and Seth had always seemed glad when he failed. Jackson breathed in as instructed, emptied his lungs halfway, then held steady.

"That's it," Radnor said softly. "Thaaaaaat's it."

Jackson released. "Ow!" He bent over, hugging his left forearm. The bowstring had slapped against it when he shot, stinging him like a wasp.

"Much better!" Yed said.

Jackson looked up. The arrow was lodged in the hay, still high and wide to the left of the target. He let out a long sigh of frustration. "But I missed again."

"Not by as much, though," Radnor insisted. "You're close. You're almost part of the bow now, part of the arrow as it flies. Once you get that, it will never leave you. There will be no pain. And you *will* reach that point, Jackson Cooper."

Jackson looked into Radnor's eyes. "Really? You think so?"

Radnor leaned close, bringing with him the smell of leather and something Jackson could only think of as completely male. "I *know* so," he said with such confidence that Jackson, despite his stinging arm, couldn't help believing him.

And so it was, as if Radnor were some kind of a fortune-teller, that four shots later Jackson felt that now-familiar warmth in his chest from the stone, a sudden sense of calm, then a shift within himself. Not in how he planted his feet or notched the arrow or held the bow. Not in how he drew the bowstring back or sighted the target or released. The change was in none of the steps, but in how he went through the entire process. He came to see it not as a series of motions but as a complete thing, mind and body together. The arrow drew closer and closer and closer still to its mark. Until finally it hit dead center, and Yed let out a loud whoop, clapping Jackson on the back so hard it almost knocked him down.

"He did it!" Yed crowed.

Radnor nodded. "I told you so. Just as it was spoken to me." He thrust his right hand up in front of his eyes, then drew it slowly away. He held the same hand out toward Jackson, palm down.

Yed did the same. He gripped Radnor's wrist at a right angle, their arms forming a T. "Hold my wrist in the same way I am holding Radnor's," Yed instructed Jackson, "and let Radnor hold yours."

"Yes," Radnor said. "This is how we begin the Ceremony of Unity, stronger together than alone, bound in the Steadfast Order." Radnor looked long into Jackson's eyes. "Join us in our quest for what is right, my friend."

"Yes," Yed said. "Join us, friend."

Friend? The word startled Jackson. Radnor and Yed wanted him to belong? Really? He looked from Radnor to Yed, then back again—father to son to father. And he could see that, yes, they really did mean it. It was as clear as the blue of their eyes.

Jackson smiled. *The Steadfast Order.* It sounded so mysterious, so magical. He shouldered his bow like

Radnor and Yed had done, then reached out and gripped Yed's thick wrist as instructed. Radnor gripped Jackson's, completing the triangle.

"Friends," Jackson said, the word as sweet as honey on his lips.

"Yes," Radnor said. "Now on to the Chamber of Initiation. So it is spoken."

"Then so it must be," Yed said.

"So it must be," Jackson chorused.

Still clasped together, Radnor and Yed led Jackson back into the torchlit Hall of the Steadfast Order.

10. Pendant Power

Later, walking back in the bright afternoon light with Radnor and Yed toward the village square, Jackson couldn't stop grinning. He'd done it! He'd faced his fear and let Yed rub the ground herb leaves on the palm of his hand, then let Radnor burn the sign of the Steadfast Order into his skin with a hot brand.

Jackson looked down at the circle with a triangle inside it. Radnor had called it "the symbol of unity and all-encompassing strength for what is right before Zallis." Jackson wasn't sure what all that meant, especially *Zallis*. They said the word with such reverence. Was it what they called God? Seemed like he'd heard something to that effect. Or had he? Memory could be such a fuzzy thing sometimes. Oh, well, it didn't matter.

Whatever Zallis was, Jackson knew there was magic in it.

Like in the stone he wore as a pendant around his neck. Yes, he was sure now. The black polished oval with the etching on it had magic in it. It had brought him to Timmra. It was what continued to give him that warm sensation in his neck and chest and the sudden sense of calm when he really needed it. And then it had protected him from pain. He'd found himself clutching it in one hand as Radnor brought the brand down onto the open palm of the other. To his continuing amazement, he had felt nothing other than pressure. Getting branded hadn't hurt. Not even a little. The magical power of the stone had apparently shielded him. He hadn't even flinched.

Radnor and Yed had both nodded. Then, to Jackson's surprise, they had bowed to him as if he were royalty. And Jackson had known that he had proved himself, just as he had with the bow and arrow. He'd passed their tests, and now he was really one of them. To show for it he had a bow and arrows of his own and a brand cooler than any tattoo he'd ever seen, even cooler than the one Seth had snuck off and gotten on his bicep last summer. That was just an eagle. It meant nothing. But his was the mark of the elite. He was the youngest member ever of the Steadfast Order, ever.

Jackson shook his head in wonder. Only in Timmra. Despite the bizarre and confusing chain of events that had brought him here, now all he could think was, What a place! So incredible, so full of possibilities. Here, time seemed to warp and twist into compacted coils that gave him ten years—no, a *hundred* years—more life for each minute. Time to become what he'd always wanted to be. In Timmra, he felt strong; he felt powerful.

Jackson smiled. He could almost feel himself getting bigger in the glow of his triumph, like a plant moved from the shadows into full sun. If only Chris and Seth—and his dad!—could see him now, walking with the Chieftain of All Timmra and Commander of the Steadfast Order, and the heir to the Chieftain's Chair. Would they ever be impressed. Tessa, too. He couldn't wait to show her how he and her father and brother had become friends.

Jackson gave Radnor a high five, then Yed, just like he'd taught them, each using the hand branded with the sign of the Steadfast Order. Jackson's grin grew even bigger. He rounded a narrow corner, head held high, only to run smack into Tessa racing in the other direction. The impact knocked Jackson back. His heel caught on a stone, and he sat down with a thump.

"Ow!"

Tessa's hands went to her mouth "Oh, Jackson Cooper! I'm sorry! I didn't see you. I've been looking all over for you. Where have you been?" She offered Jackson a hand to help him up.

Radnor stepped in front of her, a stern look on his face. "That is none of your business, Tessa." He leaned down and lifted Jackson out of the dirt with one strong pull.

"Thanks," Jackson mumbled, embarrassed that a girl had sent him flying.

But no one seemed to notice. Tessa was scowling at her father. "Jackson Cooper is *everyone's* business."

Radnor scowled right back, a threatening growl creeping into his voice. "Watch your tongue, daughter. Remember to whom you are talking."

"To whom *am* I talking?" Tessa demanded defiantly, hands on her hips. "Since you heard this voice and took the Chieftain's Chair, I don't understand you anymore. What has happened to the man I called Father?"

Yed leaned over and whispered in Jackson's ear, "Only Tessa could get away with this. This morning Radnor knocked out two of Latsi the Tailor's teeth for less." He shook his head. "Sisters!"

Jackson looked from Tessa to Radnor, Radnor to Tessa. He could understand how hard it must

be for Tessa to have to call her father Radnor and share him with so many other people.
But couldn't she see the importance of his position? Radnor had tremendous responsibility. He
was in charge of everything. The future of all
Timmra rested in his hands. Jackson wished Tessa
would just accept the facts and stop arguing. He'd
experienced enough family battles to last a lifetime.

Radnor glared at Tessa. "I am Radnor now, so I
have to take care of all my people."

A pained look came over Tessa's face. "Take care
of all your people? You call forbidding contact with
the Yakonan—"

"Stop!" Radnor roared.

A deep fierceness rose up in Tessa's eyes. "No,
you stop!"

Radnor's face went red, his fists clenched, and for
a frightening instant Jackson was sure he was going
to hit her. But instead the big man struggled to calm
himself, then reached out gently for his daughter.
"Not now," he pleaded. "Not in our time of greatest
strength. We've just initiated Jackson Cooper into
the Steadfast Order."

Tessa stepped back, a look of surprise on her face.
She stared at Radnor, her mouth hanging open. Only
after a moment did she blink and look to Jackson.
"Really?"

Jackson stood up a little straighter. He'd thought she'd be impressed. He presented his palm. "Radnor gave me a bow and arrows too," he couldn't help but add. "See?"

Tessa's eyes darted over the circle and triangle burned into Jackson's skin, the bow over his shoulder, the quiver of arrows at his side, then back to his face. "I see," she said.

Radnor cleared his throat. "Is that all? Have you forgotten your manners? Your position?"

Tessa looked away and took a deep breath. "Forgive me," she said, her voice a near whisper. She turned again to Jackson and bowed. "Congratulations on your initiation, Jackson Cooper."

Jackson beamed with pride. "Thanks!" He returned the bow.

Radnor let out a humph and pulled Jackson back upright. "Enough of this!" he grumbled. "We have to go. There's much to do."

"Yes!" Yed said. He winked at Jackson.

Radnor and Yed both started off toward the square. Jackson grinned, feeling very much like one of the guys. "Later, okay?" he said to Tessa, as if he'd always been that confident around girls. He turned to catch up with Radnor and Yed.

"Wait," Tessa said, her voice urgent. She reached out and grabbed Jackson's arm. "I need to talk to you."

"Come on, Jackson Cooper!" Radnor called. He and Yed had turned and were waiting.

Tessa tightened her grip on Jackson's arm. "No, stay," she whispered, pulling him closer to her, "just for a minute."

Jackson felt like a rope in a game of tug-of-war. Although the tension between Radnor and Tessa made him uneasy, the fact that they both wanted to be with him felt great.

"Hear what I have to say," Tessa begged. She glanced at the sky, which was growing cloudy. *"Please."*

Jackson looked into Tessa's eyes. They brimmed with emotion. Was that longing? He remembered the feel of her lips on his, so soft and smooth and warm. The flowery smell of her filled his nostrils.

"Okay," he said, and found himself trotting over to Radnor and Yed. "You guys go on," he told them, again with a confidence he could not have imagined before. But hey, he was Jackson Cooper, a member of the Steadfast Order. He was feeling downright cocky! "I'll be along in a minute or two. Just tell me where to meet you."

A spark of anger flickered across Radnor's face. But before even the faintest hint of worry could work its way into Jackson's mind, Yed broke into a wide grin. He leaned close to Radnor and whispered in his ear. Radnor's eyebrows went up in surprise.

He looked at Yed, then at Tessa, then at Jackson. A smile worked its way onto his face.

"Very well, then, Jackson Cooper," he said. "Since it would benefit our cause, I'll not be the one to stand in the way of love."

11. Their Only Hope

Jackson's face flashed hot with embarrassment. *"Love?"* he said with hushed intensity. "I don't love her!" As quickly as his denial came out, though, he knew it rang false.

Radnor threw back his head and laughed. "And I don't love roast stag!"

Flustered, Jackson stumbled over his words. "Yeah, but—uh—"

Okay, so he had come to care about Tessa a little. Okay, okay, more than a little. Who could blame him? She was, after all, the first girl ever to kiss him. She cared about him, that was obvious. And being with her felt so right. It seemed as if they'd known each other forever, as if they were meant to be. Still, he hadn't thought about it as *love*.

"But Radnor," he said. "I mean, she's—" He looked to Yed for help, but Yed just shrugged and kept grinning. "She's—well, she's your *daughter*!"

Radnor elbowed Yed. "Yes, and thirteen years old and ready to marry!"

Jackson's mouth dropped open. *"Marry?"*

"Of course," Radnor said. "All Timmran women get married when they're thirteen. It is according to the law." He laid a burly hand on Jackson's shoulder. "Go enjoy yourself, my friend, but be sure to keep your magic about you. You'll need it to tame someone like Tessa. As you've seen, she has a very strong spirit."

Radnor looked at Tessa. "Here, take him," he called out, turning Jackson toward her and giving him a playful shove in her direction. "But only for a few minutes. Get him some honey ice, there at Mook's market stall." He pointed to a canvas canopy strung across a side alley. "Cool him off, then bring him to the main gate where he is needed."

Stunned, Jackson watched as Tessa hurried to his side and clutched his hand in hers.

"Yes, honey ice at Mook's, good idea," she said, pulling him away from Radnor and Yed.

"Honey what?" Jackson said, his mind spinning with Radnor's words. *Thirteen years old and ready to marry.*

"Honey ice," Tessa said, stealing a quick glance over her shoulder at Radnor and Yed, who were still watching them go. "Here." She guided Jackson under a low-slung canopy that smelled of wet straw and mint. "Honey ice. You'll see."

A woman with plump, freckled cheeks rushed about in the small dark space, placing a large piece of wet cloth over a mound of straw. "Sorry, but I'm closing for—" She stopped when she saw Tessa and Jackson.

"Hello, Mook," Tessa said.

Mook gave Tessa a quick nod but kept her eyes on Jackson. "For such guests as you two," she said, "I'm honored to make an exception and stay open. "Would it be all right if I join you?"

Tessa looked out into the alley, then back at Mook. "Of course."

Mook bowed. "Thank you." She pulled the wet cloth back, then pushed a clump of straw to one side. Beneath was a large block of blue-tinged ice. She tapped it with her finger. "Mine is the finest, sir," she said to Jackson. "I gather it myself from the fields of ever-snow high in the Barrier Mountains. And my spice bowls"—she opened a wooden box and brought out three large oval-shaped green leaves, which she carefully placed on a small table "were carried here all the way from the South Vale."

With even strokes of a knife, Mook began to shave off thin curls of ice and place them on the leaves. "I've heard you are the one Radnor said was coming. We are blessed and honored that you'll help us. Praise Zallis."

Jackson watched but didn't see, heard but didn't listen, his mind able to focus on only one thing: the word *marry*. Was *that* what Tessa wanted to talk to him about?

Having placed a bite-sized mound of shaved ice on each leaf, Mook opened a large crock and pulled out a wooden spoon that dripped with honey. She let the thick amber liquid fall in squiggly lines over the ice. Then, with a quick twist, she folded each leaf into the shape of a bowl. She presented one to Jackson and one to Tessa, keeping the third for herself.

"Thank you," Tessa said. She glanced into the alley again, then leaned out from under the stall's canvas awning and surveyed the sky.

Jackson watched her. She looked anxious, he thought. Was she nervous about proposing to him? He shook his head. No, this was crazy. *Marry?* He was too young to marry. In Timber Grove, anyway.

He examined his honey ice, which was starting to melt. But this wasn't Timber Grove, in case he needed a reminder. This was Timmra. And here . . . well, here there were different sets of rules.

He looked over at Tessa again. She had set her honey ice down and was searching the folds of her cloak for something. She really was nice, and pretty in her own way—and yes, she liked him. But love him so much she wanted to *marry* him? The thought alone was so fantastic it made him lightheaded.

"Will this be enough in trade?" Tessa asked Mook, holding up a fine-looking white comb. "I made it just yesterday. It's one of my best pieces, from choice stag antler."

Jackson jumped. "No! I'll get it!" How many times had he imagined being with a girl and proudly paying for a treat? Hundreds, maybe thousands! He reached into his jeans pockets, only to remember he had no money or anything else to trade. His face went red. Here he finally was with a girl who wanted to—the word kept popping up—to *marry* him, and he stood as penniless as a pauper.

"Uh . . . take my watch!" he blurted out.

"You will neither pay," Mook said, waving off both Jackson and Tessa with her hand. "Who am I to charge on such a day as this, when we Timmran will rid ourselves of the troubles and once again hold our heads up high?" She raised her honey ice. "I join you in honor of our new leader, Radnor, and the Steadfast Order, which he founded!"

"In honor of Radnor and the Steadfast Order!" Jackson said, and he gobbled up his honey ice.

A wonderful cold sweetness danced across his taste buds. The ice was better than any snow cone or ice cream he had ever had. "It's really good!" he exclaimed through the mouthful.

Mook swallowed the last of her honey ice and bowed again. "How nice of you to say so." She smiled. "Now I'll show you how we Timmran tidy up after dessert." She wadded the leaf into a small ball and popped it into her mouth.

Jackson shrugged and did the same. The leaf tasted like mint and gave the sensation that his mouth was being rinsed clean. He started to say as much, but Tessa was reaching for him.

"*Finally,* Father and Yed are gone!" she said. "Come with me, Jackson Cooper!"

"But your honey ice!" Jackson said.

The thought washed from his mind as Tessa pulled him from the tent. She looked back toward the square, then turned in the opposite direction.

"This way. We need a place to be alone."

Around a corner they went, ducking into another of the narrow alleys that seemed to run like mazes through the village.

So this is it, Jackson thought. *She wants to pop the question in private!* He felt himself trembling, but didn't know if it was from fear or excitement.

He reached up with his free hand and gripped the stone pendant, wanting—no, needing—the now-familiar sensations that came from it. He ran his fingers over the etched lion. No, definitely not a lion, more like . . . maybe a dragon? And the necklace . . . He couldn't remember. Had it always been that snug? He shook the questions off. Who cared? He could feel the pendant's warm, magical power flowing into him, and once again it calmed him.

Tessa stopped and checked up and down the alley. No one was in sight, save a russet-colored chicken that squawked and strutted out of their way.

"There's so much to say and so little time," Tessa said. "Where do I begin? . . ."

She clutched Jackson's hand—the one branded with the sign of the Steadfast Order—and looked at the darkening clouds overhead as if searching there for the right words.

Jackson watched her, no longer afraid of what she was building up to. This was Timmra. He was a member of the Steadfast Order with his own tattoo and bow and arrows. He had been accepted by Radnor and Yed, Tessa's family. He had the power, the magic. Here he really could be somebody. Somebody important. Somebody famous. A hero, like Tessa had said. And then—just like in a fairy tale—the hero would claim his bride. He and Tessa would marry, and they would kiss. He leaned close, ready to start practicing.

"Tessa!"

Jackson jumped, jerking around so fast he almost fell down. Arnica was running toward them, a look of near panic on her face.

"It's starting to happen!" she shouted. "I couldn't find you at first, but Dedron—they *all* are coming." She was almost breathless as she drew close. "If we're going to do it, it's got to be *now*!"

"Do what?" Jackson asked. He took a step toward Arnica, then turned back to Tessa. "Who's coming?"

But all he saw of Tessa was the hem of her dress as she disappeared into another alley between two houses. "Don't let me down, Jackson Cooper!" she called back, her voice fading with the sound of her footsteps. "You are the Instrument, our only hope."

"Tessa!" Jackson started after her. "But I thought—" He rounded the corner. "Wait!"

The alley stood empty. She was gone.

Jackson whirled back. "Arnica, where did Tessa—"

He stopped short. Arnica was gone, too.

12. "To Arms!"

Jackson stood openmouthed in the little alley, stunned by the abrupt turn of events. "What is going on?" Everything had seemed so right only seconds before. He started once more in the direction Tessa had gone, but stopped again. The alley twisted and turned this way and that, with multiple side alleys branching off in different directions. The village was like a labyrinth. He had no idea where to look for her.

He had no idea why she had run away, either. What was it Arnica had yelled? Something about . . . Was it Dedron? It seemed like he'd heard the name before, but he wasn't sure.

And what had Tessa meant, don't let her down, he was their . . . What had she said? Their only hope? Sure, he'd gotten the idea that there were expectations of him, but still, so much remained vague in his mind. Details hadn't seemed important. All that had really mattered was how well things had been going.

But now that he thought about it, what had seemed so simple before—his picture of Timmra— was appearing more and more like a giant, complicated puzzle. And he had the distinct and disturbing feeling that all the pieces weren't even there, much less in place.

Jackson paced back and forth in the little alley, kicking up a small cloud of chalky dust. This much was becoming clear, though: Something was wrong, *really* wrong.

He'd better go find Radnor and Yed. They'd know what to do.

Full of sudden resolve, Jackson ran back past Mook's market stall and on toward the center of the village. Yes, Radnor and Yed. They'd make things right again!

But the uproar in the main square brought Jackson skidding to a halt. People were rushing in every direction. Shouts and dust filled the air. A horse whinnied and reared—eyes wide, nostrils flared. A man—as wide-eyed as the horse—cursed and jerked the reins. The horse spun, almost knocking the man down, then slammed into a market cart. It tipped over, spilling its load of corn. A little boy jumped out of the way just in time. He screamed, then cowered next to a pile of firewood, crying for his mother. A woman rushed to his side, grabbed his hand, and pulled him after her into the crowd. Confusion reigned.

Out over the chaos Radnor's voice boomed. "To arms! To arms!"

Jackson followed the sound with his eyes and saw the Chieftain of All Timmra and Commander of the Steadfast Order standing across the square by the village gate, his bow and great broadsword raised over his head. Yed stood beside him, hands cupped over his mouth. "To arms!"

"Radnor!" Jackson called. "Yed!" But there was no way they could hear him above the din. He pushed toward them, dodging around a woman herding two children before her.

"Radnor was right!" she was saying. "He said they would attack!"

Jackson stopped in alarm. "Attack? Who is attacking?"

The younger of the two children, a little girl, started to cry, big tears streaming down her face. "I'm scared, Mommy!"

"Who is attacking?" Jackson repeated.

But the woman just looked at Jackson as if he weren't there and hurried on.

His apprehension swelling with every second, Jackson spun back toward Radnor and Yed, only to bump into a man clutching a spear and an ax.

"Can you tell me what is going on?" Jackson asked. He could smell the man's sweaty fear.

"To arms!" the man shouted, his words harsh and defiant but a look of dread in his eyes at the same time. He grabbed the bow from Jackson's shoulder and thrust it into Jackson's hands, then rushed off into the crowd, calling, "To arms!"

"Radnor!" Jackson shouted. "Yed!" He could almost taste the alarm in the air now. It ran like a raw current through the agitated throng, closing in on him, too, threatening to sweep him away. He leaped up so that he could see above the crowd and get his bearings on the village gate again. There it was, and Radnor and Yed were still beneath it. Clutching his bow, he pressed on, weaving in and out, around and about, as people rushed past. Finally he forced his way through a knot of men and stood before his friends.

But Radnor's face, which only moments before had been all smiles and laughter, was now twisted in rage. "They're marching on the Council Bridge, Jackson Cooper!"

Jackson looked to Yed, hoping for a wink and a grin. This was all a big practical joke, right? Like pulling the fire alarm at school. Like the little boy in the story who cried, "Wolf!" *Tell me it is. Please tell me.*

"Treason!" Yed hissed. "We're stalked by it!"

Jackson stepped back. "Treason? *Who?*"

"The Yakonan, of course!" Radnor spit the name out like rancid meat. "Yakos! The earth shook because of them. The river level is falling. And now they attack, thinking we're helpless! But we're ready! We'll take back what is rightfully ours and then drive them from Timmra forever! It's war!"

"*War?*" The word hung in Jackson's throat like a rasp. When he was younger he'd spent hours on rainy days lining up rows of plastic army soldiers in his bedroom and then shooting them down with rubber bands and spit wads. And whenever his cousin Cody from Seattle had come down to visit, he'd always brought his toy machine guns. They'd gone out into the backyard and blasted away at imaginary enemies. He'd played war on the video games on his Sega and down at the Shop and Go, too. But that had all been for fun, nothing more than good-natured play.

"To arms!" Radnor shouted again. "Victory over the Yakonan!"

"Victory!" came a chorus of voices. "Victory over the Yakonan!"

Jackson twisted around to see at least fifty men behind him, all armed with spears, daggers, swords, axes, and bows and arrows.

"In the name of our one God, Zallis, follow me!" Radnor cried. He brandished his sword and bow over his head again. "Forward, faithful soldiers of the Steadfast Order! Victory over the Yakonan!"

"Victory!" Yed and the other men yelled. "Victory over the Yakonan!"

As one they surged out the village gate, pushing Jackson before them.

13. The Yakonan

Swords and spears glinted dully in the cloud-muted light as the soldiers of the Steadfast Order charged up to the Council Bridge.

"Form lines!" Radnor ordered, motioning with his hand. "Bowmen in the rear!"

Jackson's mind spun like a leaf ripped from a tree in a storm. He watched in a daze as swordsmen and those with spears or axes formed lines and dropped to their knees on the dusty road and in the plowed fields on either side. Bowmen stepped up behind them. Still clutching his own bow, he started to join them.

"No, here, Jackson Cooper!" Radnor pulled Jackson to the front and center. "Together we stand against the enemy!"

Yed, facing the Council Bridge, motioned angrily toward the river. "The water level has dropped even more. The Yakonan and their false songs have brought the shaking earth and this curse down on us!"

Jackson looked to where Yed pointed. The little island on which he had first found himself in Timmra had at least doubled in size from the water lowering around it. The river was now no more than a meandering channel only a few yards wide.

Radnor nodded, his mouth set in a hard, grim line. "Yako traitors!" He scanned the giant grass on the other side of the river. It swayed back and forth like dancers' hands in the stiffening breeze.

Jackson blinked in an attempt to clear his head. The slow, compacted sense of time he'd had in Timmra now seemed to have exploded out of its tight coil. So much was rushing at him so fast.

"There they are!"

Jackson startled at Yed's shout. He looked up to see the giant grass on the other side of the river parting. Out stepped at least a dozen dark-skinned people, all wearing long robes the color of clay. They walked slowly onto the road on their side of the river.

"The Yakonan elders," Radnor hissed under his breath. "Fathers and mothers of treachery."

They carried a huge drum—at least six feet across—made of what looked like an animal skin stretched over a giant gourd. Their heads were bent as they bore their load, their gray-streaked hair cascading over their shoulders, some all the way to their waists. Without a word or even a glance toward the Timmran side of the river, they approached the bridge.

Radnor's arm muscles rippled as he gripped the hilt of his sword. "It's the entire council," he said between clenched teeth. "They prepare for their chieftess, Beromed."

The Yakonan stopped just short of the bridge and set the drum down. They were now no more than thirty feet from where Jackson and Radnor and Yed stood. They took up wooden sticks with soft balls of leather at the ends.

Radnor cleared his throat and spit on the ground. "Here she comes, the leader of the enemy. Look, Jackson Cooper, there!"

Another figure was walking out of the giant grass into the open. White hair hanging almost to the backs of her knees, she moved with calm yet deliberate steps right up to the first plank of the bridge, close enough for Jackson to see the deep wrinkles in her dark face. Eyes like polished black stones, she gazed at Radnor.

Radnor held Beromed's unblinking stare. "Our treaty is split and broken!" he called out. "You've betrayed us for the last time, heathens!"

Beromed shook her head slowly. She stopped, hesitated for a moment, then took a deep breath, so deep Jackson could hear it clearly, even over the gurgling of the river. For a moment he felt sure a whole mass of people had breathed in unison. The sound was eerie, inhuman.

Beromed opened her mouth, but instead of words what came out was a noise that quivered like a wail of pain, rising into a high-pitched, warbling call that sent a shiver up Jackson's spine. He stepped back as if from a blow. What kind of people were these? Couldn't they even talk?

The wail ended as quickly as caught breath. The drummers brought their sticks down in a beat so sudden and powerful that Jackson could feel the throb of it in his chest, as if he had another heart. The earth seemed to tremble with the sound. He flinched, as did Yed and several other Timmran soldiers.

Radnor, however, stood unmoving, his face a picture of fierce determination. "We are the Steadfast Order, the Army of Timmra," he announced. He held up his palm with the circle and triangle for Beromed to see. "We have powerful magic." He cut a quick glance in Jackson's direction. "Leave Timmra and take your people with you!"

"Get out of here! Go away!" Yed shouted.

"Go away!" the soldiers chorused.

Yes, do go away, Jackson thought. *Everything was great until you weird people showed up.*

But Beromed acted as if she didn't hear, didn't care what Radnor or anyone said. She looked toward the sky, where clouds appeared to be growing thicker by the minute, and once again took a deep breath.

This time, though, instead of the unearthly wail, she sang, her voice sweet and clear, rising and falling in a steady rhythm. The drummers brought their sticks down again, not with a great bang, but in a soft, steady beat that matched Beromed's voice. Together, drum and song became music that floated up into the air like birds on a gentle breeze. It filled Jackson, resonating in his body as if he had become an instrument himself. Despite the situation, he couldn't help thinking it was beautiful, like when Tessa had sung him into a dream and danced with him at her house. Now he found himself taking a deep breath, too. A soft note began in his throat.

"False magic!" Radnor cried. "She's trying to put a spell on us. Drown it out!" He pulled his dagger and sword and began to clang them together. All around Jackson, soldiers did the same, banging swords, axes, shields, and spears, until the Yakonan music could not be heard above the din.

Beromed stopped, as did the drums.

"Silence!" Radnor ordered.

The clanging of weapon against weapon halted. Radnor pointed his sword directly at Beromed. "Enough of your heathen trickery! You've brought pain and suffering down on us, and now it's your turn to pay the price!" He glanced at Jackson again, then sheathed his sword and dagger and took his bow from his shoulder. "Pay for it ten times over, you stinking Yakos!"

"Stinking Yakos!" cried Yed and the other soldiers of the Steadfast Order.

Jackson watched tensely as Beromed turned her face into the breeze and sniffed it the way an animal would, when searching for a scent. Jackson sniffed, too. The air smelled of rain. Thunder rumbled in the distance. Beromed looked back at Radnor, returning his stare for a moment with unreadable, unwavering black eyes.

Out of the corner of his vision Jackson saw Yed ease his hand onto his quiver of arrows, fingering a shaft, and he thought of doing the same. But before he could act, Beromed sensed Yed's movement and leveled her gaze on him with such intensity that it made Jackson's breath catch. Beromed eyed Yed for a long moment, then Radnor. She nodded once and abruptly turned away, motioning to her council of elders. They picked up the drum and moved it off the road.

Relief rushed through Jackson. Beromed and the Yakonan were backing down. Radnor had won! They, the Steadfast Order, had won! And he, Jackson Cooper, had marched into battle as one of them! These strange and dangerous Yakonan—those *Yakos*—had been defeated, turned into cowards, like magic!

They could sense his power, Jackson was sure. Pride swelled in his chest. He reached up and grasped the stone pendant. The surge of warmth and confidence flowing from it into him was unmistakable now. And strength. He could feel it building, like swirling water behind a dam, ready to burst forth, to do his bidding. He felt brave, braver than he had ever felt in his entire life.

He admired the circle and triangle on his palm. *"The symbol of unity and all-encompassing strength for what is right before Zallis,"* Radnor had said. Jackson nodded. Well, right had prevailed, and he had been part of it. Tessa would be so proud. He hadn't let her down. He was a conquering hero!

Now if he could just find that girl. Where was she anyway? He looked around. No Timmran women were to be seen. He hadn't noticed before, but clearly this was a men-only army. Maybe now that the battle was over, he could go back to the village and—

"Curse you, Beromed!"

At the guttural shout, Jackson pivoted to see Radnor glaring across the bridge. Beromed and her council of elders hadn't left as Jackson had thought. They had only moved to the side and set the giant drum back down. Now they raised their sticks again as Beromed raised her hand. She motioned, and they began a strong rhythm that rose and fell, not unlike distant thunder. From the tall grass behind her a chilling chorus of wolflike cries rose into the air, and the grass began to thrash back and forth in time with the drumbeats.

"To arms!" Radnor commanded. "They prepare to attack!"

Spears and swords pointed toward the Yakonan. Axes were raised, arrows yanked from their quivers and fitted to bowstrings. Radnor and Yed both looked expectantly at Jackson.

Jackson blinked in confusion and started to ask why they were staring at him like that, when across the river the swaying giant grass parted. Out into the open marched an extraordinary parade of animals.

No, not animals, but Yakonan dressed as animals. Their costumes had been crafted with such detail as to overwhelm the dark faces of those who wore them, transforming them into wild creatures.

"Animal worship!" Yed said with disgust. "They hold beasts steadfast over Zallis."

The first in line wore a cloak of soft black fur and dragged the flat tail of a beaver. Behind it another had on the hide and head of a great stag. It stamped and pawed at the ground, tossing antlers to and fro. One limped and wore many feathers. It screeched like a hawk on the wind. Next, in slick leather, squatting and hopping, came a frog.

All moved in animal ways to the rhythm of the drums, out onto the bare dirt road on the other side of the bridge, forming a circle that rotated like a giant wheel.

"Now, Jackson Cooper," Radnor said, his voice full of hushed urgency. He held out his bow. "Make our weapons into guns."

Jackson jumped like he'd been kicked. *"Guns?"* The word came out as if he'd never heard of such things.

Both Yed and Radnor turned to him. Radnor's brow furrowed. "Yes, guns. The voice of Zallis told me that you would show your power only when it was time, and not before. Can't you see that the time has come? We need your magic weapons *now.*"

A chilling flash of realization came over Jackson. So *this* was why Yed and Radnor had been so interested in hearing about guns. *This* was what they had meant by him helping. He stood stunned by his own foolishness at not getting it before. The voice

Radnor kept talking about—the voice of Zallis—had them believing he could actually turn their bows into guns!

"Lead us to victory!" Radnor insisted.

"Yes, give us guns," Yed said. "We've heard that the Yakonan chew wild roots. It makes them crazy and they fight like madmen with their bare hands. But roots won't keep your guns' bullets from their chests. Help us defeat them in the name of Zallis and the Steadfast Order and you will be worshiped forever!"

Jackson tried to force his mind to work, to come up with a way out, an excuse. But like a frightened child caught pretending, he stumbled over his words. "Uh, well . . . you see . . . uh . . ." He looked around for a place to run. "Uh, maybe we should talk about this . . ."

Radnor's eyes narrowed. "What do you mean, Jackson Cooper?"

Jackson began to back away. "Uh . . . it's just that . . . you see, with magic you've got to have . . . uh, have everything just right, and . . . uh, I'm not sure if—"

Radnor stepped after him, a menacing look on his face. "Not sure?"

"*Father!* I mean, Radnor! Look!"

Radnor and Jackson both turned at the sound of Yed's startled voice. Across the river, walking into the center of the rotating ring, were two more dancers, each cloaked in golden fur, each with a long mane draped over his shoulders. One was a boy about Jackson's age. The other . . .

Jackson squinted, trying to get a better look. The other was a girl. She tossed the hair back from in front of her face, a cascade of blond. Jackson shook his head. No, it couldn't be.

Another dancer—a small child—ran with bouncy little steps from the tall grass. She was dressed in the same golden fur as the boy and the girl, and she joined them in the center of the wheel.

It simply could not be.

But it was.

Tessa and Arnica.

14. Vengeance

Radnor's face went pale. "They've kidnapped my daughters!"

Words rose in Jackson's throat as he tried to scream a warning: *"Tessa! Arnica! Run! Get away!"* But what came out was less than a whisper. Tessa was slipping her arm around the Yakonan boy's waist. And he around hers. Together they took Arnica's hands, and they all moved with soft, cat-like steps.

"Wh—What?" Radnor stuttered in disbelief. "They're dancing with the Yako!"

Jackson watched dumbfounded as Tessa smiled up at the boy, then raised on her tiptoes and kissed him on the lips. He gasped and turned to Radnor and Yed, desperate for them to come to his rescue, to tell him that what he was seeing wasn't real.

"It's evil magic!" Yed said between clenched teeth. "The Yakos have bewitched Tessa and Arnica!"

Radnor's face had turned red with fury. He grabbed Jackson and dragged him up onto the wide planks of the bridge. "Give us guns *now*!" he commanded. "We will kill him. We will kill all the Yakos!"

"Kill the Yakos!" Yed echoed, charging up behind Jackson and Radnor.

The soldiers of the Steadfast Order surged forward, too. "Kill the Yakos!" they yelled, shaking their weapons in the air. "Kill them!"

"No, Jackson Cooper!"

It was Tessa. She was walking quickly toward the bridge. "Don't listen! I love my family, but this time they're wrong."

"*Wrong?*" Radnor bellowed.

"Yes, *wrong*!" Tessa said. She moved up onto the bridge and stopped no more than ten feet from her father. "The Yakonan aren't to blame for the troubles. They love the Vale."

"It's not the Vale, it's Timmra!" Radnor poked his bow in the air, punctuating each word with an angry thrust. "And there is no place in it for the Yakonan. They've stolen our good life from us, and now they've stolen you and Arnica. They are low and vile. They smell like the animals they worship."

"They worship one god, just like we—"

"They're heathens!" Radnor cut in. "I know. The Voice of Zallis has told me. But anyone can see it in their dark, shifty eyes! They're the cause of the earth cracking open, of our precious river water draining away."

"They didn't do that!" Tessa insisted. "It's the—"

"You can't believe what they say!" Radnor shot back, pointing an accusing finger at the Yako boy, who had edged closer.

Yed jumped in. "They're murderers! They killed our mother!"

"That's not true!" Now it was Arnica, rushing up beside Tessa, her eyes glassy with tears. "It was the sickness last winter that—" Her voice broke, but she swallowed hard and went on. "It was the sickness that took Mommy."

A pained look came over Radnor's face. He shouldered his bow and knelt, reaching out for Arnica to come to him. "Yes, little one, it was the sickness that took your mother, but it was the Yakonan who brought the plague on us."

"No they didn't!" Tessa said. She held Arnica to her side. "When Mama's fever got so high I went to their village."

"You *what?*" Radnor stood, eyes flashing.

Tessa's eyes flashed right back. "They gave me herbs to help cure her," she said, her words rolling out in a quick stream. "They said we have to join together—Timmran and Yakonan—to defeat the illness, just as Musa the Yakonan and Grier the Timmran joined in defeating the Baen in the ancient days. It's the *Baen* that has caused all this, not the Yakonan. It's trying to escape from the Underworld. Jackson Cooper was sent to fix the Shaw-Mara so that we can keep the Baen from coming back. He is the answer to our Prayer Song. He is the Instrument of Panenthe. He is—"

"No!" Radnor cut in. "Listen to me, not to heathen myths and lies of this pagan god, Panenthe! It is the one *true* god, *Zallis,* that protects us from evil. That is why *He* sent Jackson Cooper! I know. Zallis speaks to me!"

"It is the Baen's voice you are hearing, Father," Tessa said, "not the voice of Zallis."

"Stop!" Radnor boomed. "I won't hear it! It's sacrilege!" He turned to Jackson. "Do as Zallis promised. You are the One, the Liberator, who will lead us to victory! Give us guns so we can break the evil spell that puts unspeakable words in my daughter's mouth!"

"Yes, Jackson Cooper!" Yed said. "Break the Yako spell!"

"I'm not under any spell!" Tessa insisted. "Neither is Arnica. We're here because we want to be, under our own free will, to prove to you that Timmran and Yakonan can still dance in harmony, that we can work together to fight the Baen." She moved closer—now only an arm's length—and peered intensely into Jackson's eyes. "Do I look to be under a spell? You should know."

Jackson's mind spun in confusion. He wasn't a mind reader, but he wasn't a fool, either. No, she didn't look under a spell; it didn't sound like evil magic was forcing words she didn't want to say out of her mouth. But maybe . . . maybe the Yako magic was so powerful she actually thought she believed what she was saying. These Yakos were strange, frightening people. Just look at the boy now standing right behind Tessa, staring at him as if he would kidnap him, too.

"The Yakonan tried to help," Tessa said. "They're good people." She motioned to the Yako boy. "*He* is a good person. His name is Dedron, and we are in love and want to marry."

The word *marry* hit Jackson like a fist in his chest. He staggered back, mouth hanging open, air coming in short, shallow breaths. Tessa was to marry *him*. Radnor had said so.

"*Love?*" Radnor roared, pulling his bow from his shoulder again. "Marry? A Yako? It's against the will of Zallis!"

"False magic!" Yed cried. "The Yako wants to hold her hostage in his evil spell! *False magic!*"

"False magic!" the soldiers of the Steadfast Order shouted. They began banging weapon against weapon again.

Tessa winced at the clanking din. She scanned the sky, fear showing plainly in her eyes. The clouds had begun to swirl as if whipped by some gigantic hand. Thunder rumbled, deeper, more cavernous than before.

"See what they can't see, Jackson Cooper," Tessa pleaded. "In the name of Panenthe, in the name of love and harmony, help us. Now is the time."

"Yes, now *is* the time! In the name of Zallis, do something!" Radnor demanded.

Jackson's stomach twisted, his head swam. He began to tremble, then shake. How could Tessa talk of love when she'd turned so quickly from him to this—Jackson looked at the boy called Dedron—this *Yako*? How could she—

"Jackson Cooper."

The words began low in Dedron's throat, like a soft growl, so much like an animal, full of wildness. "Jackson Cooper." He stepped up beside Tessa, his dark eyes locked onto Jackson's, a penetrating stare that seemed to pry Jackson open, expose his very soul. Like a rabbit caught far from its burrow, like doomed prey, Jackson froze, his mouth suddenly wordless, his mind blank.

"Listen to me," Dedron said. "After the Baen was defeated, the earth opened up and swallowed it, leaving only the tips of two of its fangs that had broken off in the battle. With those two fang tips Musa and Grier made this."

Not taking his dark eyes from Jackson's, Dedron reached under his cloak and pulled out what looked like two short bone flutes lashed tightly together with a leather thong.

"We call it the Shaw-Mara."

A rich amber color, the twin flutes shined as if polished smooth by the touch of many hands.

"Its notes, if blown together by a Timmran and a Yakonan, are the only thing that can stop the Baen from returning."

Even as Jackson recoiled from Dedron's unnerving stare and animal voice, he felt himself being pulled toward the Shaw-Mara, wanting to touch it, to hold it.

Dedron held the Shaw-Mara out toward Jackson. "But the Baen has somehow snuck his power into the Vale and silenced it. No matter how hard we blow, it makes no sound. Help us."

Jackson's hands began to twitch, to ache for the flute.

"Use your power to fix the Shaw-Mara."

A sudden spasm wrenched Jackson's fingers out straight. His bow fell with a clatter onto the bridge planks.

He started to reach out for the Shaw-Mara.

"Don't listen, Jackson Cooper! It's a trick! He's trying to capture your soul, too!"

Yed's voice jolted Jackson as if he had been in a trance. Relief flooded him, along with deep fear and anger. He had almost been bewitched by Dedron. It *was* evil magic. He *did* have Tessa and Arnica under a spell.

"Destroy him and set my daughters free!" Radnor commanded. He scooped up Jackson's bow and thrust it at him. "Use the magic power Zallis gave you!"

But Jackson waved the bow off. Yes, his power—not the bow but the incredible black stone. How could he have forgotten, even in all the turmoil? Jackson reached up and grasped the pendant. Strength, more than ever, much more, instantly flowed into his hands. He glared at Dedron. "Leave me alone!" he said, his voice coming out like thunder.

"Jackson, please," Tessa begged. "The Baen!"

Dedron held the flutes out toward Jackson. Jackson looked down at the fingers and palm that only moments before had been pressed against

Tessa's back. They looked calloused and capable, but oddly unreal, more a foreign object than part of a human body. Anger swelled and rose in Jackson's chest at the sight of them.

"Listen to your heart," Dedron said. "Don't be afraid."

"*Afraid?*" The word was like a spark set to gunpowder. Jackson's hands began to tremble with concentrated force. It surged into his fingertips, vibrating with a sensation like electricity ready to release. He held his hands up and shook them in Dedron's face.

"You're the one who'd better be afraid!" he shouted, and a tiny spark shot from the tip of his left index finger with a sizzle.

Radnor's scowling face snapped into one of shocked wonder. "Your hands! But I thought—Is that a gun?"

A collective gasp filled the air. "A gun!" Several of the Timmran soldiers standing nearby stepped back, eyes fixed on Jackson's hands as another spark—longer this time—shot out of his fingertips. As if in answer, lightning flashed across the sky and the rumble of thunder surrounded them.

"You don't need that kind of power, Jackson Cooper." Dedron stepped out in front of Tessa, who stared wide-eyed at Jackson, clutching Arnica to her side.

The stone pendant flared on Jackson's chest, now radiating power like a sun. All of Jackson's fingers began to spark. Foot-long arcs of jagged light crackled in the air, answered again by lightning and rumbling thunder from above. "Don't tell me what I need!" he boomed, and leveled his fingers on Dedron. He felt all-powerful, invincible, filled with righteousness.

"Yes, Jackson Cooper!" Radnor urged, his voice hot in Jackson's ear. "Break the Yako spell on my daughters."

"Show them the power of Zallis!" Yed said into the other ear. "Show them the power of the Steadfast Order!"

"But you don't understand," Dedron said, for the first time a hint of fear seeping into his voice. "It is Panenthe who sent you, not Zal—"

"Shut up!" Jackson bellowed, and the next thing he knew he had erupted, lunging at Dedron, seizing him around the neck.

"No, Jackson Cooper–Jackson Cooper!" Arnica cried. She rushed forward with Tessa, who was shouting, "Stop!" Tessa grabbed Jackson, digging her fingernails into the backs of his hands.

In one quick motion Radnor was yanking her away, corralling both her and Arnica in his massive arms. "You don't know what you're doing! You're under a Yako spell!"

Jackson's hands tightened on Dedron's neck. It was as if they had a mind of their own. "Break the spell on Tessa and Arnica!" he demanded.

Dedron struggled in Jackson's grip, wrestling to get free. "But I didn't put them under a spell!"

"Liar!" Jackson thundered. He tightened his grip even harder. Dedron gagged. "Heathen liar!"

"Jackson, stop!" Tessa screamed.

Arnica cried, "You're hurting him!"

"Pl—please . . . ," Dedron choked out. "In the name of Panenthe . . . I can't . . . breathe. . . ."

For an instant a memory flashed across Jackson's mind. Seth had gotten mad and punched him in the stomach once, doubling him over. Jackson had lain in the playground dirt, gasping for breath, thinking he might die, feeling like he wanted to. Now a momentary rush of regret filled him and his grip loosened just a little. In that second Dedron twisted desperately to get free, his elbow slamming into Jackson's forehead.

It was as if lightning had struck, then thunder, knocking Jackson back. For a moment patches of light and dark were all he could see. Intense pain shot through his head, jabbing, gouging. Then something inside him snapped, and all the hurts and humiliations of a lifetime swelled up from deep in his center, shrieking, "No more!" A mighty force burst from the stone pendant into his hands, increasing the power there tenfold, a hundredfold. As if possessed,

Jackson lashed out in a blind fury, his hands now like clubs, and caught Dedron square across the face.

Tessa and Arnica both screamed as Dedron fell back, a gash beneath his eye. Blood spurted from his nose.

Tessa clawed frantically at Radnor, fighting to get free. "Stop, Jackson Cooper! Stop!"

Eyes as fierce as they were wild, Jackson ripped the Shaw-Mara from Dedron's hands.

Dedron grabbed for it. "You'll destroy us all!" His voice was full of terror. *"Listen to me!"*

Jackson screeched like a banshee. "Stinking Yako!" He shoved Dedron back with such force that his head made a loud thud when it hit the planks of the bridge. "You're the one who destroyed everything! And now I'm going to destroy you!" He crammed the Shaw-Mara into his jacket pocket, backed up a step, and leveled his hands at Dedron's chest. Shaking with rage, tears streaming down his face, he concentrated all the hate and vengeance that had seized him into his fingers and aimed it right at Dedron's heart.

"No!"

Tessa's cry penetrated the wrath that gripped Jackson's soul, and something within told him to listen.

But he was already past letting go.

15. Battle Cry

Like a demon unleashed, a terrible crackling blast ripped the air as huge, jagged bolts of lightning flashed from the ends of Jackson's fingers. At the same instant a bridge plank only a fraction of an inch from Dedron's neck exploded into splinters. Jackson's hands jerked up and back as if kicked, his arm slamming into his forehead. He staggered, stunned, the acrid smell of sulfur burning in his nostrils. The thunder of the explosion echoed in his ears, then shifted into a deep rumble.

Dedron lurched to his feet, wiping blood from his face. He looked around, dark eyes wide with fear, as the rumble continued. "Panenthe save us," he said in a trembling voice. "This isn't the work of the Otherworld, but the *Under*world. You—*You*, Jackson Cooper, are a servant of the Baen!"

Jackson stared in a daze at his tingling, quivering fingers as—despite all reason—the rumbling echo grew louder, vibrated deeper, as if sinking into the earth beneath the bridge.

Or as if coming from the earth itself.

The notion felt disturbingly familiar to Jackson, yet he couldn't remember why. He tried to wipe away the haze that clouded his mind, but with no success. He felt as if he were standing in a dark dream, awake and yet unable to move out of it and into the light, unable to see what would normally be clear.

"Jackson Cooper!" The voice was full of awe. Jackson turned to see Radnor. "Your magic—the power of Zallis—is great indeed!"

"Yes!" Now Yed was before him, a wide grin on his face. "Look, they're shaking with fear!"

Jackson looked to where Yed pointed. On the other side of the river, the Yakonan had retreated to the edge of the tall grass, many on their knees as if begging for mercy.

Only their chieftess, Beromed, had rushed forward and was pulling Dedron off the bridge and back to his people, even as he resisted.

"Dedron!" Tessa cried out from the bonds of Radnor's arms. Tears spilled down her cheeks. "Dedron!"

Arnica started to cry, too. "What is happening?" she begged. "I'm scared!"

Radnor clutched his daughters even tighter to him. "Don't worry. The evil spell will wear off soon. Look at the Yakonan. They know their false magic is defeated. Jackson Cooper has captured their heathen relic. They're afraid. They're cowards." Eyes mocking, he jeered at Dedron and Beromed. "Yes, fear the Steadfast Order and all Timmran! Fear Jackson Cooper. Fear the power of Zallis as it poises to destroy you!"

"Three cheers for Jackson Cooper!" Yed shouted.

"Yes, three cheers!" Radnor commanded.

The soldiers of the Steadfast Order moved in close around Jackson, weapons raised, pumping them in the air, shaking them at the Yakonan.

"Jackson Cooper!"

Their faces swam before Jackson's eyes.

"Jackson Cooper! Jackson Cooper!"

More joined in, until it became a chant.

"Jackson Cooper! Jackson Cooper! Jackson Cooper!"

Jackson turned in a slow circle, the cheers for a moment drowning out the rumbling echo under the bridge.

"Lead us, Liberator!" Radnor said. "Lead us to victory!"

Jackson blinked, then blinked again. Did this mean . . .? Yes, he'd done it. He'd been afraid but hadn't run. Instead, he'd stood his ground and fought—*really* fought—for what was right, and he'd won. He gripped the pendant where it hung from the necklace, now snug around his neck, and felt yet another surge of power pass from it into his pulsing hands.

"Jackson Cooper! Jackson Cooper! Jackson Cooper!"

A smile slowly worked its way onto Jackson's face. They wanted him. Him, Jackson Cooper, the Liberator, sent by Zallis, whose name they chanted. They wanted him to lead them to victory. Then surely the spell the Yakonan had put on Tessa would break and she'd see him for what he truly was—a hero, just like he'd dreamed of being. He lifted his hands—his powerful, magic hands—over his head.

"Forward!" Jackson shouted his battle cry. "In the name of Zallis, fight for Timmra, fight for what is—"

A great thundering roar came from under the bridge. Jackson looked down to see the river churning in frenzied whitecaps beneath them, the mud quivering. The timbers of the bridge creaked and groaned, then trembled.

Fear flickered in Yed's eyes. "The earth is shaking again!"

"Everyone off the bridge!" Radnor ordered, picking up his daughters, one under each massive arm.

Tessa fought to break free. "Dedron!" she called again. "Dedron!"

Yed grabbed Jackson's elbow. "Come on, Jackson Cooper," he urged. He pulled Jackson with him as he followed his father and the soldiers of the Steadfast Order back off the bridge on the Timmran side. "Stay with me."

The roar came again, even louder than before, building in volume, swelling. The earth under Jackson's feet shuddered, and he was knocked to his knees.

The bridge convulsed and heaved upward. With a huge splintering crack it shattered, then fell down into a great fissure that was opening beneath it in the center of the river. The water rushed in after the timbers and boards, sending billowing clouds of harsh, sulfurous steam into the air.

Jackson staggered to his feet and stumbled back, coughing and covering his nose and mouth as a hot fog engulfed him, burning in his nostrils. "What—What is happening?"

But no one answered. All were retreating from the riverside, even Radnor. He sheltered his daughters with his cloak, though Tessa still struggled to escape.

"Dedron! Dedron!" she screamed.

THE EYE OF THE STONE

With a deafening boom the fissure in the river grew into a gaping abyss. From the chaos of breaking stone, raging water, and billowing steam came a terrible, cavernous roar so wild and fierce it made the hair come up on the back of Jackson's neck. He stared in helpless horror as out of the abyss climbed a huge beast, dreadful beyond imagination.

16. The Baen

Leather-skinned like a lizard, yet with the maned head of a lion, the monstrous creature rose up on powerful back legs to twice the height of a grown man. The hooked claws of its toes sliced into the hard earth like knives into butter. It glared around with blazing red eyes.

"The Baen!" Tessa cried at Jackson. "You've freed the beast!"

"No!" Radnor shouted as the creature whipped its long spiked tail about behind it. "It's Yakonan evil. They conjured this up. Kill it, Jackson Cooper! Kill it with the gun of Zallis!"

"Kill it!" Yed said, backing away, his eyes wide with fear. "Kill it *now*!"

The beast unfolded sinewy fingers, each tipped with a hideous, curled, daggerlike talon. In his mind

Jackson ordered his hands to do as Radnor commanded—to use the power of the pendant to send a bolt of lightning crackling from his fingertips, slamming it into the beast's chest, crumpling this nightmare into a smoking cinder and saving the day once more. *Be a hero.*

"Kill!" Radnor shouted again. "I command you!"

But Jackson's body would not respond. He stood petrified with fear, unable to move, his hands hanging limp at his sides.

Radnor shoved Tessa and Arnica at Yed. "Hold them!" He yanked his bow from his shoulder and shook it in front of Jackson. "It shoots only arrows!" he said. "See?" In one swift movement he fit an arrow to the string, aimed, and released. It zipped through the air and buried itself deep in the beast's shoulder.

With a snarl the beast wrenched the arrow free and threw it to the ground.

"We need the fire of Zallis!" Radnor said. "We need it now!"

Still, Jackson could only stand and stare.

Radnor spit in disgust, then fit another arrow to his bowstring. "To arms, soldiers of the Steadfast Order!" he commanded. "Kill the Yako beast! Kill it and defeat the Yakonan forever!"

Arrows and spears filled the air. One struck the bone above the beast's right eye, the shaft splintering. Most bounced harmlessly off the beast's armor-like hide.

Radnor threw his bow to the ground and drew his sword. "Blades and spears!" he yelled above the confusion. "Surround it. Attack!"

With a wild battle cry Radnor charged, a wave of soldiers rushing behind him. The beast roared. Its muscles rippled into tight bands. It slashed out at Radnor. He leaped to the side, barely escaping the cruel talons. Whirling, he brought his sword down, hacking off one of the beast's fingers, leaving it wriggling on the ground in a pool of black blood. The Baen screeched in pain.

Radnor shook his sword in the air. "We've got it! Kill!"

The soldiers of the Steadfast Order swarmed in. One thrust his spear at the beast's underbelly. With a blinding swipe the monster broke the spear shaft as if it were a toothpick and raked the man's chest with its claws. The man fell back screaming, bright red with blood. An instant later another soldier was pulled into the beast's grasp, his shriek of terror coming to an abrupt end as the beast bit down on his neck with jagged yellow fangs.

Jackson shook his head, trying to clear away the shock of violence in which he found himself swimming. Another wave of soldiers surged forward, slashing with their swords, thrusting with spears, hacking wildly with battle-axes.

Snarling, roaring, the beast lashed out again with its great claws and spiked tail. Men spun and fell, twirling partners in a dance with death. The ground turned crimson with blood.

"Deliver us!"

Jackson turned to see Yed release Tessa and Arnica and drop to his knees. Tears streamed down his cheeks as he bowed his head and clamped his hand over his eyes, then drew it away. "In the name of all that is Steadfast, I beseech thee, Zallis. . . ."

At first Tessa seemed not to notice she'd been freed. She was squinting into the foggy melee, a look of anguish on her face. For there was Dedron, moving like a cat across a sagging beam that had wedged into the top of the abyss when the bridge had collapsed. He scrambled up onto the Timmran side, grabbed a fallen spear from the ground, and began fighting the beast alongside his enemies.

"Dedron!" Tessa cried, and ran toward him.

"Tessa!" Arnica sprinted after her sister. "Don't leave me!"

Tessa scooped up a sword. Together she and Dedron lunged at the beast, stabbing at its side. The beast whirled on them, its tail whipping across the earth like a giant club. It caught Arnica right across the chest. Her piercing scream stopped mid-breath as she was slammed to the earth.

"Arnica!" Radnor's fierce cry seemed to break Yed's trancelike prayer. He sprang to his feet, dagger drawn, and charged forward, flinging himself onto the beast's back just as his father did the same. Both drove their weapons in deep. Dedron leaped up beside them, now jabbing with only a splintered spear as a weapon.

The beast screeched and slashed at its tormentors. In a split second all three lay crumpled on the ground. Tessa rushed to them. The beast reared up and glared down at her with evil red eyes.

"No!" With all his might Jackson concentrated his power on the beast, aiming at its underbelly. A crackling blast echoed above the clash of battle, ringing in his ears as lightning flashed from his fingertips.

In the instant of that flash, Jackson was knocked to the ground as if struck by a huge fist. His chest stung like fire. Around his neck, the chain gripped him in a stranglehold. He reached up, groping for the pendant. The necklace broke and fell into his hand, no longer a chain of gold, but now a snake coiling through the eye of the stone. It hissed at him and flicked its tongue over the etched drawing—no longer a lion, nor a dragon, but now the perfect likeness of the beast.

Jackson gasped and dropped them both. They hit the ground and exploded into tiny shards. The power drained out of Jackson's hands and body like water out of a sieve. "But—" Jackson whimpered, a deep chill rushing in where strength had been before. "But I thought—"

The beast snarled. Jackson jerked his head up to see it still standing, ready to attack. Only now it had turned its blazing gaze on him. It stalked toward him with murder in its eyes.

Terror gripped Jackson like an iron fist. "Help!" he cried, scooting backward on the ground.

"The Shaw-Mara!" Tessa screamed. "It has to be—"

The beast roared, drowning out the rest of Tessa's words.

But Jackson had heard enough. The Shaw-Mara. Tessa and Dedron had said it had to be blown in order to keep the Baen away, that he could somehow fix it. He had thought it was a Yakonan lie, but now . . . He fumbled desperately in his jacket pocket for the twin flutes he had taken from Dedron. He yanked them into the open.

The Baen roared so loudly at the sight of the Shaw-Mara that Jackson was sent sprawling again. He rolled to his knees, raised the Shaw-Mara to his lips, and blew. Nothing happened. Not even a hint of a note came out. Frantically, he whacked it against the ground as if he could beat notes out of it. Then he blew again and again with all his might.

Nothing.

Looming over him, the Baen rose up for the kill, talons dripping blood, great fangs glistening. Blind with fear, Jackson spun and scrambled to his feet, only to trip over a fallen soldier. The Shaw-Mara flew from his hand and sailed through the air in a terrible, graceful arc.

"No!" Tessa screamed. "Save it!"

But the Shaw-Mara had vanished over the edge of the abyss.

The Baen roared in fury, then leaped. With a shriek of raw horror, Jackson clamped his hands over his eyes and cowered on the bloody ground. Trembling violently, he waited the unendurable moment before the first white-hot flash of agony, the cruel beginning of what would surely be his gruesome end.

17. Into
the Abyss

As abruptly as it had begun, the chaos of thundering violence ended. Jackson opened his eyes and looked down at his body. No blood, no great gashes, no broken bones. For some reason he could not fathom he was untouched. The Baen was gone.

"Thank God!" His breath came in a great rush of relief. He jumped up. "It didn't get me! I'm—"

Jackson's words of celebration caught in his throat. Bloody soldiers littered the ground, some pleading for help, others lying still—too still—eyes open and unmoving. He turned away from their glassy stares, only to see Tessa hovering over Dedron, then Arnica, then Yed, then her father.

"No!" she wailed. "No!"

Dedron lay moaning, blood at the corner of his mouth, on his forehead, coming from his nose, smeared across his cheek. Beside him Arnica curled limp like a worn and discarded doll, her chest jerking with ragged little breaths. But it was Yed and Radnor who looked the worst, their shirts red with blood, their faces ashen.

"No!" Tessa yanked her cloak from her shoulders and pressed it over her father's chest, then her brother's. The blood soaked through in seconds. Yed trembled, then went slack. "Please, no!" she cried. Radnor began to thrash about. *"Please!"*

Although horrified, Jackson still could not pull his eyes away. Radnor gasped, and his entire body went rigid. Then, in a slow sigh, his breath left him.

Tessa sat back on her heels, moaning. "Daddy. Yed. Why? Why couldn't you see what was so plain to me?"

"Are they . . . ," Jackson ventured. "Are they both dead?"

Tessa spun on him, eyes wild with grief, and lashed out. "You did this!"

Jackson stepped back as if slapped. "I—I didn't hurt them. It was that—that *thing* that—"

"No!" Tessa cut him off, her voice shaking with fury. "I thought you were the Instrument, sent by Panenthe in answer to our Prayer Song. I thought you would fix the Shaw-Mara and everything would be fine again, and Father would be able to see the love between Dedron and me, the love possible between Timmran and Yakonan, like in the old days between Musa and Grier. But the Baen tricked my father into thinking he was hearing the voice of Zallis, then he sent you to free it. This was all it needed, your act of hate. And now . . . now my father and my brother are dead and the Shaw-Mara is gone!"

"But—But—Wait," Jackson said, pleading for understanding. "You've got me wrong!"

Tessa stared at him with pure malice in her eyes. "The Baen will find the Shaw-Mara and make it part of itself again. Restored to its full strength, it will come back and force us to be its slaves or die"—her voice broke on the sharp edge of her grief and rage—"because of *you!*"

"It wasn't my fault," Jackson said, whining now. "Everything happened so fast and—I didn't know!"

"*Didn't know?*" Tessa cut the air violently with her hand. "Your power came from the Baen. You were its slave, a servant of evil. If you didn't know that, if you didn't have the courage to face it, then you are nothing but a . . . a *stupid coward!*" With that she turned her back on Jackson and collapsed in great heaving sobs.

A stupid coward. A servant of evil. Tessa's words lodged in Jackson's heart like a whole quiver of arrows, and with a rush of deep sorrow he knew it was true. The stone pendant was the Baen's, and the Baen had tricked him into wearing it and then doing its bidding. He hadn't meant to cause so much pain, but that didn't change the fact that he had. He could have listened, could have asked questions, could have sought the truth.

Jackson looked down at his shaking fingers, at the circle-and-triangle sign of the Steadfast Order branded on his right palm. But the simple fact was that he hadn't even tried to get at the truth. He'd been too consumed with his own desires. And so, in a fit of power-crazed fury, he'd become what he'd always hated in others—cruel—and had unwittingly done the work of evil.

Tears welled up in Jackson's eyes. "I'm sorry," he moaned, sinking to his knees. "I'm really sorry."

"Regret erases *nothing*, you fool."

The voice was weak and raspy, but the words were razor sharp. Jackson looked over to see Dedron roll onto his side. Dedron coughed. The sound ended in a cry of pain. Jackson had a sudden surge of nausea.

"Get out of my way," Dedron said, pushing himself up onto his knees, "and I'll show you how to"—he started toward the edge of the abyss, moving in broken lurches, like Jackson's cat had done after being hit by a car—"how to do what has to be done."

Tessa reached out to stop him. "No, Dedron," she pleaded. "You're hurt. You can't."

A flash of fury shot through Dedron's eyes. "If I don't go get the Shaw-Mara, who will?"

Lower lip trembling, Tessa looked around at the dead and wounded. "I don't know," she said, her voice quavering. "But I've lost so much already." Tears streamed down her face. "I couldn't stand it if—"

"I'll do it," Jackson said.

Dedron and Tessa both turned to him and stared.

Jackson blinked, trying not to look as shocked as he felt. It was as if something inside him, something other than himself, had willed the words to come tumbling out of his mouth. And then there came more.

"I'll get the Shaw-Mara back, and I'll make it play again."

"This is not crazy. This is not crazy." Jackson eased his feet over the edge of the abyss, trying to convince himself that he was not rushing into a doom of his own doing. "I'm not going to die."

But every time he looked beyond the first foothold, his breath caught in his throat and his heart sank. The dirty fog rising up out of the bottomless shadowy depths looked too much like wicked tongues. The jagged rocks around which the fog swirled jutted out too much like fangs. The odor of sulfur mixed with decay stung his nostrils too much like the breath of something unspeakably foul. The entire abyss gaped open too much like a giant hungry mouth that could snap shut at any moment and devour him.

Just as the Baen could do. Echoing above the sound of the river cascading into the abyss, the Baen's roars sent cold fingers of fear running up Jackson's spine. He lost his resolve and turned back, only to find Dedron right in his face.

"You said you'd do it, so do it!" Dedron barked.

Jackson searched the Yakonan's fierce dark eyes. He wished he could imagine successfully pulling off this daring rescue he'd gotten himself into. But even if he did somehow manage to find the Shaw-Mara before the Baen did, and even if he did get back out of the abyss alive with it, what in the world had possessed him to promise he could fix the thing? He had no special power other than what the Baen had given him—evil power—and now even that was gone.

Tessa knew. She sat with Arnica cradled in her arms, staring at him with a cold mixture of anger and despair in her eyes. Although she said nothing, Jackson knew what she was thinking. The same cutting words still rang in his ears: *Stupid coward.*

Jackson looked back down at the first foothold. "One step at a time," he found himself saying in a shaky whisper. "You can do it." He took a ragged breath, tested the foothold yet again, found a good handhold, then lowered himself into the abyss.

18. Shadowlands

The grimy fog quickly enveloped Jackson with its damp, smelly fingers. Only a few feet into the abyss, he looked back up to find that he could no longer see Dedron. A feeling of complete and utter aloneness swept over him. He cringed and leaned in against the rocks, which was a mistake. His foot slipped out from under him, his hand tore loose, and in the blink of an eye he was sliding down the steep slope.

Flailing with his hands like a bird gone crazy, Jackson clawed wildly at anything that could stop his quick acceleration. His foot caught on an outcropping of rock and flipped him. He tumbled out of control, head over heels, his life flashing before his eyes—a sad parade of failure.

Then he hit and water was everywhere, so icy it sucked the breath right out of him. He struggled to the surface, to find himself being swept downstream in the new river channel that had formed in the bottom of the abyss. He gulped air through lips already beginning to tremble. The water was *so* cold. He had to get out. He began working his stiff arms and legs, swimming as hard as he could for the wall of the abyss.

He had gained only a couple of feet, though, when he heard the roar of cascading water ahead and looked to see foaming waves suddenly dropping out of sight. A waterfall! He flailed with frantic yet leaden strokes for a nearby boulder that jutted above the flow. A standing wave actually pushed him in the right direction, banging him into it. He grasped for a handhold.

But the rock was too slippery, and Jackson's fingers too numb and weak to hold on. The powerful current ripped him loose and, in the next instant, swept him over the edge.

For a long, horrifying moment Jackson knew neither up nor down, only a violently tumbling world. His lungs ached for air, but the pounding of powerful watery fists drove him under. Darkness closed in, and with it an odd sense of calm detachment, as if he were watching it all on TV.

So, Jackson thought, *this is what drowning is like. I'm going to die. Pretty stupid of me. What would Chris and Seth say?*

He shook his head. *No, I shouldn't die, it's my birthday. Mom promised she'd make double-fudge chocolate cake. I love that stuff, especially with extra icing.*

Jackson almost smiled at his silliness. How could he think about double-fudge chocolate cake at a time like this? He was drowning.

But then somehow he was on the surface again, coughing up water just as the river had coughed him up, and thinking only of survival. His strength was gone, though. He began to sink again when his foot brushed against something solid and, by reflex, he pushed.

The next thing Jackson knew he was wallowing about in a shallow eddy. He staggered up, slipped back, then finally struggled out of the river and collapsed in a heap on a sandy beach. Shivering violently, he thought of his Trailblazers jacket. It was back at Tessa's house, right where he'd left it. A powerful wave of hopelessness and utter exhaustion swept over him. With a weak groan he rolled onto his side and curled up into as small a ball as possible. In seconds darkness descended like a blanket on his brain, and he knew nothing . . .

. . . until he woke with a start, heart pounding. Sweat streaked his face, soaked his chest. His throat ached as if it were on fire. He had never felt so completely parched. He sat up, desperate for water, only to find the river no longer there. It was now nothing more than an empty ditch of rock and powder-dry dust.

"What?" Jackson struggled to his feet, gaping at the river bottom. All that water—gone, vanished. As was the putrid fog that had filled the abyss. In its place, acrid smoke swirled on a hot blustery wind. Dirt kicked up into small dust devils. One of the whirlwinds raced at Jackson, throwing grit in his face.

Jackson shielded his eyes with his hand and stumbled up the riverbank. The wind eased a bit and he peered through the haze. Smoldering pits dotted the floor of the abyss, and odd-shaped pillars of stone. He squinted at the closest one, examining its knobby surface.

Jackson's stomach lurched. The stone appeared to have been sculpted into the shape of a man, but twisted into grotesque contortions—arms and legs broken and bound, mouth open in a silent scream. Jackson searched the horrible, terrified-looking face. There was something disturbingly familiar about it.

A movement atop the man's head caught Jackson's eye. He looked up to see a shadowy figure perched there, darker than the surrounding gloom.

A new surge of fear rose in Jackson's throat. He turned and began to trot quickly away from the specter.

Another shadowy figure stirred atop another pillar. In the dim light Jackson could see the outline of a face—half human, half bird, with empty eye sockets. The creature cocked its head as if listening for an intruder, then opened its hooked beak and pierced the air with an unearthly screech.

Jackson broke into a run, sprinting as if his feet had sprouted wings. For wings were what now filled the air—great horrible wings, flapping like muffled hand claps, as all around him hundreds of screeching shadow creatures lifted upward. They joined into a dark mass and dove after him.

Jackson ducked when he felt a whoosh near his head, but not soon enough. A shadow creature's tail slapped against his neck, sending a stinging pain shooting down his back. He cried out and clutched the wound. When he pulled his hand away, he found it smudged with dark soot.

A second then a third shadow creature attacked, whacking Jackson across the shoulder, the head. Pain coursed through him like lightning. "Stop!" he screamed. "Get away from me!" He tried to dodge the attacking shadow creatures, jumping behind one of the stone pillars, then spinning as he ran. But their marks were crusting up on him like dried mud, slowing him. If this kept up, he wouldn't be able to move at all.

A whimper escaped Jackson's lips. *So this is how the pillars were formed. They don't just look like petrified people, they actually are!* At the thought of such a thing, he stumbled and fell. Three shadow creatures swept in on him, pummeling him with their wings, leaving streaks of darkness on his shoulders, his head, down his sides.

"Help!" he screamed. "Somebody help me!" He scrambled to his feet and ran in a blind, cowering panic with his arms over his head. "Please! I don't want to die!"

The earth began to shake, the pits in the ground to rumble and spew fire. Great clouds of sulfurous smoke belched into the air, engulfing Jackson, gagging him. The shadow creatures shrieked, then suddenly whirled—as if on command—and disappeared into the smoke.

"Thank God!" Jackson gasped. Choking, coughing, he staggered around a bend in the abyss . . . to find the Baen.

19. Darkness and Stone

Although no more than twenty feet away from Jackson, the Baen hadn't seen him yet. It was fixed on bashing a boulder the size of a bus with its powerful spiked tail. Pieces of rock flew in every direction, pelting the abyss walls. Whirling around, the monster dug furiously at the scrabble with its huge talons like a dog after a bone.

No, not after a bone. After the Shaw-Mara. Jackson could see the twin flutes wedged between the canyon wall and the boulder. *The river must have washed it there before drying up,* Jackson thought. Although it was out of the Baen's reach for the moment, it wouldn't be for long at the rate the beast was turning the boulder into gravel.

The Baen snarled and leaped around to the far side of the rock. It lashed out with its tail once more, then lowered its head and tore away with its claws.

It was Jackson's chance, he knew; maybe his only chance. He closed his eyes and forced images into his head: Him rushing behind this side of the boulder and scooping up the Shaw-Mara before the beast knew what was happening. Him racing to the cliff and shooting up it like a rocket, handing the Shaw-Mara to Dedron. Tessa, forgiving all, throwing her arms around him, kissing him like she had before, the hero. Arnica, too. The Shaw-Mara somehow miraculously fixed. Dedron and Tessa blowing it, the Baen forever gone. . . .

But that image vanished instantly when Jackson opened his eyes and looked again. With ribbons of muscle and tendon flexing beneath leathery skin, its great mane bristling and fangs bared, the Baen slashed at the rock with enough strength to rip him in two.

Get out of here! every fiber of Jackson's being screamed. *Climb like a madman, then run as if hell itself were on your heels.* Because it would be, he knew.

Then another voice rose up in Jackson's mind: Tessa's, also urging him to flee. *"Yes, turn and desert us, Jackson Cooper!"* Her words stinging like wasps. *"Run, you stupid coward, you servant of evil!"*

Jackson reached up and touched his chest, wishing he had the stone pendant despite the wickedness it had carried. Just for a moment, to give him the power to do what should be done. Then he'd get rid of it. Promise. But he needed it now, really needed it. His arms hung limp at his sides like wet noodles; his legs felt like jelly.

"I'm sorry," Jackson whispered as if Tessa and Dedron and Arnica could hear him. "I just—I just can't do it." He turned to flee but immediately tripped and went down with a clatter on loose stones. The Baen's head shot up, its fiery red eyes locking onto his.

Instinct took over. Jackson sprang to his feet and bolted for the only place he could see to hide— between the boulder and the abyss wall. The Baen bellowed and charged to cut him off. Jackson dove, barely making it in time.

The beast slashed at Jackson with its cruel talons. Jackson scrambled back to get out of its reach. Jagged fangs bared, the beast gnashed at the rocks. Its foul breath hit Jackson like a hot wind. The smell of rotting garbage burned in his nostrils, so wretched that for a moment he thought he would vomit. He pushed himself back even farther into the crack.

The Baen leaped around to the other side of the boulder and bashed it with its spiked tail, each blow thunder in Jackson's ears. A hailstorm of rock shards rained down on him. Jackson lunged around in the opposite direction as the talons lashed in at him again, one catching a pant leg, slicing it like a razor.

The beast slammed its tail even harder. A zig-zag crack appeared in the boulder. It was only a matter of time, two more blows, maybe three, then— Jackson shuddered at the hideous possibilities. He was trapped. There was no way out. Unless . . .

Jackson twisted around in the crack, and there it was, the Shaw-Mara. He scooped it up. This was what the Baen wanted, right? Maybe if he threw it really far and the Baen went after it, then that would buy him enough time to get away. Maybe, just maybe, it would work.

The beast slammed its tail with even greater feroc-ity. The crack in the boulder widened. Jackson raised the Shaw-Mara. He had no choice. Tessa and Dedron and Arnica would understand that, wouldn't they? He cocked his arm to throw.

At the sight of the Shaw-Mara in Jackson's hand, the Baen let out a wild hiss, then reared back and rammed its monstrous head right at Jackson. The power of the blow knocked the boulder a foot far-ther from the abyss wall, and the beast lunged . . . only to grind to a halt, wedged between boulder and cliff, inches short of its prey. Face to face with the beast, Jackson looked into a huge, flaming red eye only an arm's length from his own. There, in the depths of the cavernous black pupil, he saw his father, crusted in stone, looking back at him, deep sadness etched on his face.

"*No!*" Jackson cried out in wrenching anguish as everything became terribly clear. The Baen hadn't tricked just him. It had tricked his father, too. In a time of weakness, when his father was out of work, it must have tempted him with irresistible visions of Lady Luck, fantasies of wealth beyond his dreams. It must have played on his father's desperate longing to provide for his family, and so captured his soul. Under the Baen's spell, his father had then bound the stone to Jackson's neck with the gold chain, and so bound Jackson to the Baen.

From deep in the core of Jackson's being rose a wild, defiant scream. *"Let us go! Leave us alone!"* He lashed out with all his might, stabbing the twin ends of the Shaw-Mara directly into the Baen's eye.

A sound like shattering glass split the air. The Shaw-Mara let out a sharp whistle, while in the Baen's dark pupil, the stone encrusting Jackson's father cracked and began to crumble. The Baen shrieked in pain as black blood streamed down its face. It lunged at Jackson again, driving itself even farther between the rocks, so tightly now it couldn't move.

Jackson spun and scrambled out from behind the boulder, clutching the Shaw-Mara to his chest. The stone pillars cracked and crumbled before him, just as his father's had.

"Jackson Cooper–Jackson Cooper! Up here!"

Jackson looked up to see the sulfurous smoke which had filled the abyss earlier now parting, revealing the upper rim. Sticking out over it was a small head. Jackson's face lit up. "Arnica!" She was OK! "Look!" He held up the Shaw-Mara. "I got it!"

As if calling to her, too, the Shaw-Mara let out another sharp whistle. Jackson gawked at it for a moment before it hit him. He must have broken the Baen's hold on the flutes when he'd stabbed the beast in the eye. "It's working again!" he shouted. "We can—"

From behind the boulder came a gruesome snarl and the grinding, ripping sound of the Baen struggling to get free. In a heartbeat Jackson stuffed the Shaw-Mara into his pocket and was climbing as fast as he could up the abyss wall toward Arnica.

Below him a series of thunderous blows echoed. Jackson looked down over his shoulder to see the Baen lashing with its powerful back legs and tail. Chunks of rock flew in all directions. The beast wriggled, jerked back once, then twice, then—with a great roar—a third time. The boulder shifted, and the Baen was free. It clawed at the rubble, but then stopped. With a screech of rage it looked about, then up.

Adrenalin pulsed through Jackson's body as the Baen sprang after him, clawing its way up the side of the abyss. Jackson strained, scrabbling for footholds and handholds, then leaping for the next.

"Hurry, Jackson Cooper–Jackson Cooper!"

There she was, Arnica, closer now.

"Here!" came another voice. It was Dedron, reaching down for him. "Give me your hand!"

"Come on!" Even Tessa was rooting for him now. "You can do it!"

So close, Jackson stretched for them.

"Look out!" Arnica screamed.

A terrible black talon jammed into a crack in the rock just below Jackson's feet. In one swift motion he yanked the Shaw-Mara from his pocket and hurled it upward. It bounced against the stone face of the abyss, arced outward, and began to fall. Dedron lunged and snagged it, almost tumbling into the abyss himself. Tessa grabbed him by his cloak at the last instant and hauled him to safety.

"Blow!" Jackson shouted.

"But—" Arnica began.

The beast hissed in rage, its hot stinking breath raking Jackson's ankles like fire.

"Blow!" he commanded. "Together! *Now!*"

Tessa and Dedron put their mouths to the Shaw-Mara—a Timmran and a Yakonan, united—and blew. Two notes rolled out of the twin flutes, blending in powerful harmony, building, swelling, cresting into a great wave of pure shimmering resonance so loud it shook the earth.

With a great rumble the abyss began to close. A huge slab of rock just to Jackson's right broke off, barely missing him. It slammed into the Baen, ripping its talons from their hold. With a horrendous yowl the beast fell backward, plummeting into the narrowing canyon below.

"Jackson Cooper–Jackson Cooper!"

Jackson leaped up with all his might—for Arnica, for Dedron, for Tessa. But the gap of sky above him narrowed to a thread, then disappeared as darkness and stone bore down upon him.

20. A Different Kind of Strength

Crushing pressure came at Jackson from all sides. Pain drilled into him, shooting through every part of his body. He cried out, but the sound of his agony never left his mouth, muzzled by the powerful grip of the collapsing abyss. Like a huge and cruel fist, the stone walls mashed his arms to his sides, squeezed his eyelids shut, wrung the breath from him like water from a rag, all the time pulling him into a descending spiral.

Down, down, past a three-headed dog that lunged at him, snapping viciously with yellow fangs, tearing at his flesh.

Down, down, where lightning ripped open blood red clouds and wasps swarmed out, stinging his hands, his face, his eyes.

Down, down, bitter cold sinking its icy fingers deep, freezing Jackson's tears of anguish to his face.

Down, down, the heat of a thousand suns scorching his skin, parching his lips.

Down, down, the strangling force of the abyss growing more vast than the center of gravity, where light itself could not have escaped, beyond anything Jackson ever imagined endurable.

And yet in the next moment the pressure eased, then released in a sudden rush. The pain was gone. And Jackson opened his eyes to find himself lying curled in a pool of golden light. It streamed in on him through a narrow opening between dark stone walls.

"What . . . ?"

Dazed, he stood and stumbled into dazzling brightness.

"Where . . . ?"

Above the limbs of green firs and leafless alders, the sun was breaking through a blanket of gray clouds. He stared, dumbfounded.

"But how . . . ?"

Slowly, a smile worked its way onto Jackson's face. Who cared how? He was alive! Alive and well and back in Oregon! He looked down at his hands. The circle and triangle of the Steadfast Order were gone. He checked his watch. As if on cue, it began to tick off the seconds. It was still the same time—4:43. He checked the date—November 13. Yes! That was still the same, too, his birthday.

"Yahoo!" Grinning like a kid in an ice-cream shop, Jackson clambered down the rocky slope to the base of Cougar Butte. As he entered the trees a squirrel chattered. He looked up to see the little animal glaring down at him from a nearby fir branch.

Jackson waved. "Hey, squirrel! How's it going?"

The squirrel flicked its bushy tail from side to side. It chattered again, then leaped from the limb onto the trunk, its tiny claws scratching in the bark as it scurried out of sight to the far side of the tree.

"See ya later!" Jackson shouted. He took a deep breath of the cool, clean air. It felt so good to be back in Timber Grove. Maybe the place wasn't perfect, but it wasn't so bad, either.

Just look! he thought as he made his way to Cougar Creek and headed downstream. Everything seemed to sparkle like new in the brilliant sunlight flooding the forest, as if the whole world were celebrating his birthday. Trees, rocks, ferns, even the moss-covered logs glistened. If he squinted, it looked like everything was strewn with diamonds.

Jackson's grin grew wider. They'd have to change the name from Cougar Creek to Diamond Creek. That would be so cool to live in a forest full of diamonds. He'd be king of it all, King Jackson! He stood up straighter as he walked with big strides. "Make way!" he proclaimed. "Here comes King Jack—"

A distant yet very familiar sound cut Jackson short. It was the growl of his father's pickup truck laboring up the hill toward their house. *Becky!* She was home alone. In a split second his glee vanished and he was racing toward his house, leaping over logs, plowing through ferns, sprinting out of the forest.

Tires splashed in the pothole at the bottom of the driveway as Jackson squeezed through the hole in the back fence. He dashed around the woodpile and across the yard, pumping his arms as fast as he could.

Brakes squealed. The engine sputtered, then died. The truck door creaked open, then slammed shut. Jackson bounded up the back porch steps and burst into the kitchen.

Footsteps crunched on the front sidewalk as he rushed through the living room and around the corner, then took the stairs two at a time. He made the landing at the top, to find Becky waiting for him, eyes sparkling with excitement.

"I found this old football helmet of Dad's in the attic and— Hey, how come you're so wet?" She pointed at his clothes. "Where have you been?"

From below came the rattle of the storm door opening. "Never mind," Jackson said. "Forget it, OK?" He slipped past her into his bedroom and turned to shut the door.

"But Jackson!" Becky pouted. "I just wanted to know—"

She went silent as a muffled voice, low and gruff, drifted up from the living room: "Emma, get off the couch!"

A wild mix of emotions raced through Jackson at the sound of his father's voice—relief, concern, anger, fear. His father was alive, not crusted in stone, not locked in the eye of the Baen. But obviously he wasn't in the best of moods, either. Each of his words came out with a sharp edge to it.

"I said, get off the couch!"

Jackson stood holding his breath as the deep thump of his father's footsteps crossed the living room, paused for a moment, then continued into the kitchen. The refrigerator door slammed, then a cabinet drawer. Jackson winced. A chair scuffed, then the back door banged shut. Jackson shook his head. *Having a beer on the porch steps, no doubt. Not a good sign.*

Becky put the football helmet on over her pigtails. "I'm going to play in my room," she murmured sadly.

Jackson nodded. "Good idea." He started to close his door again when a faint sound drifted into his ears, echoing, then shifting. A note . . . No, two . . .

"Hey, did you hear that?" Jackson whispered after Becky.

She turned and took off the football helmet. "Hear what? Daddy?"

"No." Jackson held up his hand, signaling her to be quiet. "Listen." The notes came again, a little louder this time, definitely two of them, played in harmony. Light and airy, yet clear and perfect, they floated in the air, lingered for a moment, then faded slowly away. "There!"

Becky stared. "I don't hear any—"

"There again!" Jackson cut in as the twin notes sounded once more, clearer now, deep and rich. And Jackson knew—it was Tessa and Dedron, playing the Shaw-Mara. Their music filled him with sudden hope, like a March breeze that carried hints of spring. He walked to the edge of the landing and looked down the long flight of steps.

"I have to talk to Dad," he said.

And just as quickly as he'd said it, he was imagining it: down the stairs, through the living room and the kitchen, then out the back door. To sit with his father and talk man to man about what had happened, about *why* it had happened. He needed an explanation. He needed to give one, too.

After all he'd been through, what would be so hard about that? He'd faced the Baen, recovered the Shaw-Mara, then thrown it to Dedron and Tessa. He'd done the right thing, at least partly making up for the harm he'd caused in the Vale.

"You're crazy, Jackson-boy!"

Becky's words cut into Jackson's fantasy like a knife. His shoulders slumped. A hollow pit formed in his stomach. And just how did he think he was going to pull this off? Wave a magic wand over his father and himself and make everything all right? Say a few words and erase the weakness of character, the sad longing in them both? Undo the resulting betrayal? The anger? The violence? The wrong? Sprinkle forgiveness and understanding all around like confetti?

A sharp, humorless laugh escaped him. While he was at it, why not just go ahead and open the lumber mill back up, too? Sure, jobs for everyone! And then they'd all live happily ever after, just like in a fairy tale!

Jackson shook his head. *Right.* If only life were even close to being that simple. The cold hard truth was that talking to his dad would be like walking out onto thin ice with lead boots on. At any instant what seemed solid could crack and give way, plunging them both into frigid black water.

A panicky thump started up in Jackson's chest. He looked back into his room. It would be so much easier just to go in there and shut the door. It would be so much easier to lock himself in and everything else out. It would be so much easier to pretend none of this had ever happened. After all, a person could *die* in icy water.

As if they were being played right there in the narrow hallway, the twin notes sounded once again. They resonated with such intensity that the air, the walls, everything, seemed to vibrate in harmony with them.

Even Jackson—first his fingers, then his hands, his arms, his entire body, especially in his chest—vibrated. He reached up and touched the spot where the stone pendant had once rested. Now beneath his shirt he felt only the thump of his heart, slowing from its panicky pace, growing steadier, stronger with each beat.

Not strong like the power of bulging arms or a broadsword or a magic pendant or a gun. It was a different kind of strength, hard to define, but swelling and rising in him just the same, filling him with something bigger than himself, bigger than anything he'd ever experienced. It was as if he were being filled with light. And it made him feel . . . maybe the word was *brave.* Not comic-book brave, like some kind of superhero. Not without fears. He had no illusions. But maybe brave enough to at least face those fears.

Jackson stood up straighter and looked back down the stairs. No, this wasn't how he was going to die. It certainly wasn't going to be easy, but this was how he was going to live.

"You can do it," he whispered to himself. "You can."

With a deep breath, he took the first step. . . .

Acknowledgments

I've told myself a *billion* times (almost) not to exaggerate, but it really does seem like it has taken me *forever* (almost) to finish this book. (I started it in 1988.)

It is truly *not* an exaggeration, however, to say that *lots* of people have helped me out along the way. What follows is a partial list, with sincere apologies to anyone whom, in the chaos of fifty-two rewrites—yes, fifty-two, really!—I may have left out:

Debbie, Kelsey, and Amy Birdseye; Jean Naggar; Regina Griffin; John and Kate Briggs; Margery Cuyler; Frances Kuffel; Ann Manheimer; Gary Hines; Anna Grossnickle Hines; Betsy Partridge; Martha Weston; Jane Yolen; Robert McKee; John Anderson; Kelly Monahan; Molly Switzer; John Otto; Susan Lowell; Ross Humphries; Jeremy Meyer; the Corvallis-Benton County Library; Anderson's Sporting Goods; the Oregon Department of Employment; and Juan and Amadeus.